MIDNIGHT ECHO

Issue 15 - November 2020
www.australasianhorror.wordpress.com/midnight-echo/

First published in 2020 by The Australasian Horror Writers
Association in conjunction with David Schembri Studios.

I0584532

Like us on Facebook
Follow us on Twitter

Produced in Australia

AHWA

DAVID
SCHEMBRI
STUDIOS

ACKNOWLEDGEMENTS

Production Team:

Guest Editor
Lee Murray

Convenor
Alan Baxter

Cover Art/Layout
Greg Chapman

Proofreader
Céline Murray

The Staff Would Like to Thank
Midnight Echo's fantastic contributors, readers, and fans.

CONTENTS

††AHWA Flash Fiction Competition Winner 2019

†††AHWA Short Story Competition Winner 2019

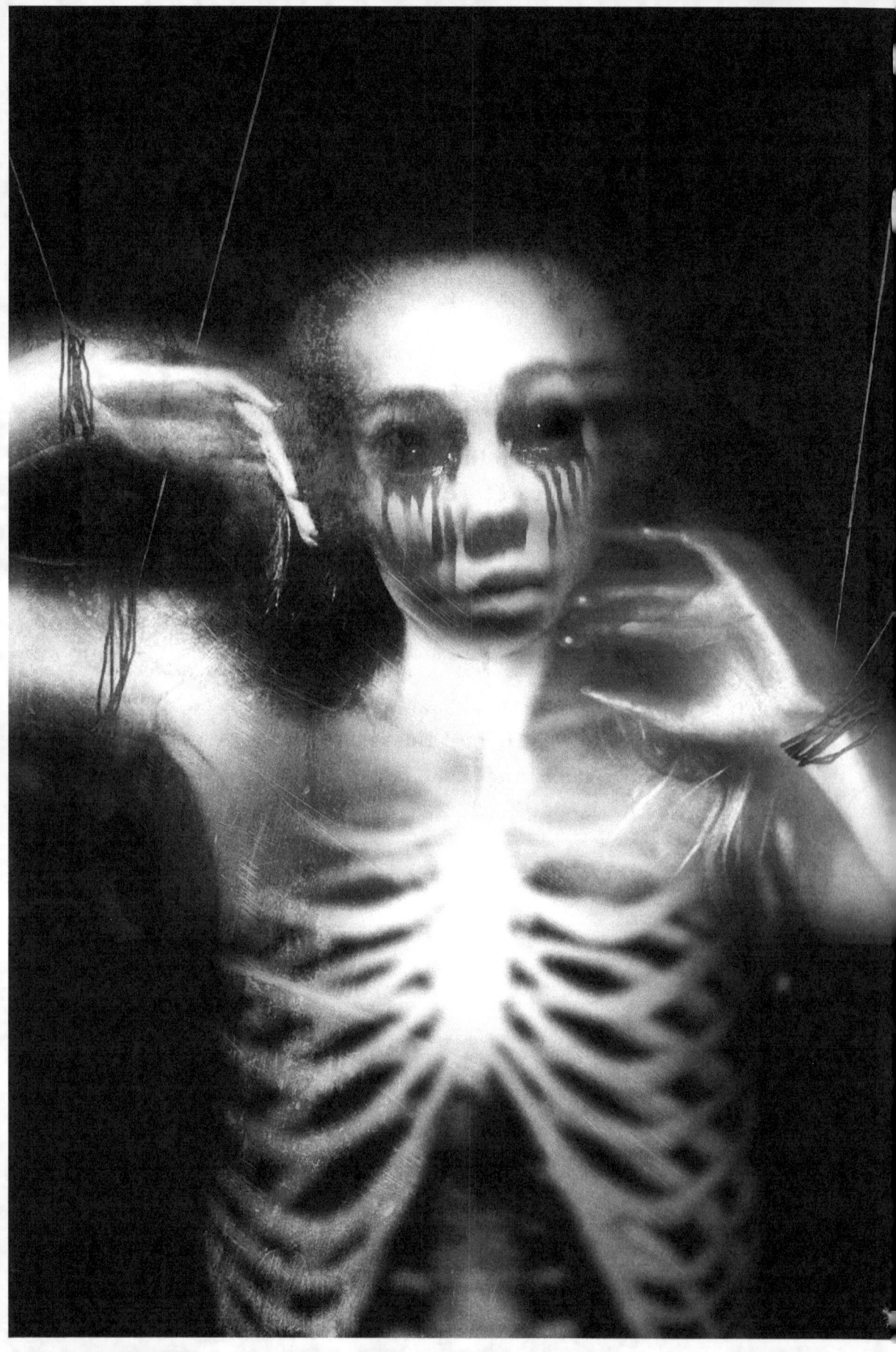

EDITORIAL

In the seminal novel that launched a genre, Mary Wollstonecraft Shelley wrote, "There is something at work in my soul, which I do not understand." With this single sentence, Shelley cuts at the reason that so many of us embrace dark fiction. Because when we read and write dark fiction and horror, we are seeking to expose the inexplicable, to explore and make sense of the fantastical and the macabre at work on our souls. In 2020, with humanity confronting challenges on a near-apocalyptic scale, there has been a lot to make sense of, and, it appears, a concurrent surge in our consumption of horror.

It was in this environment that the AHWA offered me the role of guest editor of the annual magazine Midnight Echo. This year's issue, #15, would include a print digest version as well as the usual digital offerings. I didn't hesitate. As a long-time member of the Australasian horror community, and a former vice-president, committee member, and mentor, not only did curating the magazine offer a way to pay it forward to a community that has been integral in growing my career, but there was clearly a huge demand for horror as a means of processing all that we were experiencing, both as creators as consumers.

The Australasian horror community responded with what I believe was a record number of submissions, including significant numbers from my Kiwi compatriots. It was a privilege and a pleasure to read this quiver of dark stories, poems, and essays, from both emerging and established writers. The submissions straddled every subgenre, from horror comedy to classic retellings and steampunk horror. There were quiet moments of unease, and stories that shocked with their brutality. Supernatural fantasies and real-life horrors. I sifted and sorted. With so many excellent entries, and a tight budget, something had to give; I would need to make some gnarly decisions, disappointing some colleagues and passing on some otherwise excellent pieces. But with an anthology, the whole should always be more than the sum of its parts, so I looked for works which not only resonated with strong themes and vibrant writing, but which would also sit well together. Representing a variety of styles, story structures, and settings. All seeking to expose those unspeakable things at work in our souls. With these aspects in mind, I made my selections.

Our desire to provoke the uncanny began with our earliest experience of darkened bedrooms, when we dared to challenge the monster that dwelled under our beds. What might happen if we were to slip our foot out from under the covers, for example? Dangled it like bait in the darkness… It is fitting then, that we open this fifteenth volume of Midnight Echo with "The Bone Fairy" by Martin Livings. In this story, a precocious child dares to manipulate the tooth fairy, to tease and test "the shadows as sharp as little teeth" that striate the floorboards on the night of a full moon; it's a dare which, once entered into, cannot be taken back.

There are times, though, when a parent will step forward, switching on the light to chase away the shadows, or, as is the case for the protagonist in "Tolerance to Iron" by Jason Franks, one might even venture into the darkness, a hero to confront the little men that lick their lips and watch our children while they sleep.

Some of us survived those early encounters by a sniff, like the near-miss neatly outlined by Melanie Harding-Shaw in her tiny tale of unquiet and weirdness, "A Second Chance", and likewise in Rebecca Fraser's "Keep Walking", where the ballad's dogged cadence brings home the poet's message of betrayal and denial.

Others among us gained a measure of control, and Juleigh Howard-Hobson's haunting little poem, "A Charm to Sicken" lays out the recipe in devilishly easy steps. Similarly, Nikky Lee delights with "The Dead May Dance", a vengeful tale of the occult that ought to make the dead turn in their graves. Yet supernatural powers often come at a cost, the dark secrets a constant threat to those who wield them. Indeed, in David Schembri's "My Claire" and J.A Haigh's "Trace a Circle" the protagonists, on the one hand a gnarly grandpa, and the other a young girl, each face just such a danger, in two very different and yet equally enthralling stories on the same theme.

As we grew, our nightmares refused to stay under the bed, but instead walked the world with us, worked, and sometimes slept, beside us as Alissa Smith reveals in "A Little Spoon", a chiller of a tale told in two hundred words, and 2019 AHWA Flash Fiction Competition Winner. Also, on the topic of monsters who walk among us, Deborah Sheldon shatters readers with "Carbon Copy Combustibles", a science fiction story set in a technology driven near-future that is overrun with hubris. This bite-sized thriller terrifies with its possibility, with Sheldon's main character, everyman Charlie Pomeroy, recognisable as living inside and alongside all of us. Then Tom Dullemond offers another stomach-churning eventuality in a story centred around the hostile takeover of a pizza chain.

In a world ravaged by COVID-19, "Colony Collapse" is as shocking as it is relevant.

It is not always us who go looking; sometimes Horror *chooses* Her disciples. She seeks us out with stories that howl into the night, that worry at our souls, and demand to be heard, as Anthony Ferguson explained when he returned his manuscript: "I immediately thought, wow! That is a horror story right there." He was right: delivering up his skin-curling tale of revenge-served-cold in "Brumation".

Perhaps Mary Shelley rose from her grave to travel centuries and oceans and whisper dark nothings in Joanne Anderton's ear, prompting Anderton to stitch together her story "Hidden Armature". After all, didn't Shelley keep her lover's heart in a box after his death? Anderton uses a contemporary setting, but her bizarro tale is equally horrifying.

Not everyone makes it out alive as Jay Caselberg reminds us in "The Reaping", a lonely poem echoing faintly of Lovecraft and exquisite in its brevity. And finally, the worst kind of hell: those who are doomed to live their lives on repeat, hurtling through space with only tantalising glimpses of the life outside. Stuart Olver's "The Midnight Song", winner of the 2019 AHWA Short Story Competition is just such a tale, reminding us that some fates are indeed worse than death.

I'd like to thank the AHWA for the opportunity to shape this year's issue, and especially to my colleagues for trusting me with their dark delicacies. In my opinion, Midnight Echo #15 is one of our best issues yet.

As Alice Cooper put it: "Welcome to my nightmare; I think you're going to like it."

Lee Murray, September 2020

A FINAL MESSAGE FROM THE PRESIDENT

This will be my final edition of *Midnight Echo* as President—and committee member of the Australasian Horror Writers Association (AHWA).

It's a bitter sweet feeling because when I first joined the Association way back in 2013 as a general committee member I never imagined that I would end up being at the helm.

The last seven years—in particular the last three years—have been very challenging, to say the least. But I don't want to dwell on that, instead I want to celebrate what the AHWA does best and that's help promote Australasian horror writers in various ways, including through the publication of *Midnight Echo* magazine.

One of the joys of my role has been putting these issues together and to think that we've now reached our 15th issue is a credit to the tenacity of the AHWA, despite the odds.

This is the first print edition of *ME* since Issue 10 in 2013. What you hold in your hands is not just a magazine, but a collection of wonderful imaginers. People dedicated to storytelling. Horror fiction can, sometimes, be much maligned, but it holds an important place in the world. Especially the current world we live in, which consists of a seemingly unstoppable virus and so-called leaders who have willfully forgotten how to be decent human beings.

Horror holds a mirror up to the world after all.

You're in safe hands with Guest Editor, Lee Murray, a gifted New Zealand author and former AHWA Vice-President. We couldn't think of anyone else more suited to edit this issue.

If you're an AHWA member thank you for your continued support to help keep vital projects like *Midnight Echo* going. Without your financial support, it simply might not exist.

If you're not a member and have purchased a copy out of curiosity, thank you. We hope you enjoy it and go out of your way to make your fellow horror afficianados know.

I also want to thank my fellow AHWA Committee members. Truly, I could not have done this without you. As always, I wish the AHWA the very best for the future.

Greg Chapman, September 2020

AUSTRALASIAN HORROR WRITERS ASSOCIATION

AHWA

THE BONE FAIRY
BY MARTIN LIVINGS

The first time was an accident, I swear to God. But sometimes once is all it takes. One mistake, and you're damned.

I lost a baby tooth when I was eight. It came out in a bloody smear, tiny and pearlescent like a seashell. I showed it to my parents, but they didn't pay any attention to me; they were too busy caring for Benny, my baby brother, who'd monopolised them ever since he'd come screaming and shitting and puking into their lives six months earlier. The only time they paid me any heed was when they caught me screaming at him or pinching him or threatening him.

"He's your brother," they'd scold me. "Your little brother. You have to protect him."

I didn't want to protect him, though. I didn't want him at all.

I stormed back to my room, stamping my feet as hard as I could, and threw the tooth at my wardrobe. It bounced off the mirror and landed on the carpet. It looked small and sad and pathetic there, ignored and alone—exactly how I felt. Then Cleo, our crabby old cat, materialised from wherever she'd been hiding in my room and pounced on the tooth. I shooed and kicked her out, dodging the vicious claws that swiped at me as she retreated into the hall, hissing. Cleo hated me, hated everything and everyone pretty much. Especially Benny, the new interloper. My parents actually closed the door of his nursery at night, for fear of her scratching or smothering him or whatever. I wouldn't have minded if she had. Serve him right.

Once Cleo was banished, I picked up the tooth and, like a good boy, I put it under my pillow. I knew the routine.

The next morning the tooth was gone, and a fifty-cent piece had taken its place. The Tooth Fairy had visited. That made me happy. Someone was paying attention to me. To *me*, not Benny.

It felt good. I wanted more. But my other teeth were rooted solid in my gums. Not like the one I'd lost, which had been wobbly for weeks. I wondered if maybe I could knock one out, but the thought terrified me. I didn't like pain, or blood. No, I didn't want to knock my teeth out, not for fifty cents, not for fifty dollars. Not my teeth.

Not *my* teeth.

That gave me an idea, one both as simple and as ridiculous as only an eight-year-old could come up with. Cleo had killed a mouse months earlier, torn its head clean off and left it on the doorstep, a gift, or a warning. Dad had taken the head and buried it behind the house, under the jacaranda tree at the back of the yard. Mum said he should just throw it in the bin. But he'd insisted, said it was a living thing and deserved respect.

One afternoon, when Mum was taking care of Benny and Dad was still at work, I went into the backyard and dug it up. The bugs and worms had done their jobs on it, so all that was left was a bare skull. I ran it under a tap, and it came up shockingly white. I looked at it closely, looked at its empty eye sockets, the eerie curves and hollows on the sides of its head. And, most of all, I looked at all the sharp little teeth embedded in its jaw. So many teeth. I imagined getting fifty cents for each of them. I smiled, baring my own teeth at the skull, as if taunting it.

My *teeth are fine right where they are, thank you very much.*

But those teeth, these tiny dagger-like teeth, they had an appointment with the Tooth Fairy.

I secreted the skull underneath my pillow that night. It was so small, I barely felt it there as I slept, dreaming of being special. Being noticed.

The next morning, it was still there.

I was disappointed—but stubborn. Night after night, I tucked the skull beneath my pillow, hoping that it would be taken, that I could fool the fairy. Night after night, nothing.

Until one night, the night of the full moon. The first night.

That swollen moon shone its sickly yellow light through my bedroom window, making the shadows as sharp as the little teeth under my pillow. I took a long time to fall asleep that night, and when I finally did, I had horrible dreams, dreams of tiny knives pricking at me, crab claws scratching my toes, hungry, hungry.

When I woke the next morning, the skull was gone.

I looked at the rumpled sheet beneath my pillow, frowning. There was no coin there, no gift from the Tooth Fairy. Instead, there was just a small silver-grey lump, covered in a thin layer of white corrosion.

There were also teeth. All the teeth. Left behind. Rejected.

I stood beside my bed, still half-asleep and confused. I looked at the lump of metal, at the teeth. Then I understood, with the kind of logic only a child could have.

It didn't want teeth.

It wanted bone.

* * *

The first time was an accident. The second was not.

I fished a chicken bone from the bin. I cleaned it off thoroughly, and I placed it under my pillow when I went to bed.

The following morning, the drumstick bone was still there. Then I remembered the mouse's skull, and the light in the room the night it had vanished, that sickly yellow light of the full moon.

I put the bone away with the tiny mouse teeth and lump of metal, and I waited.

The night of the next full moon, I brought the bone out again, placed it under my pillow, and went to bed. But I couldn't sleep, I just couldn't. I imagined the fairy coming, dressed in shimmering cloth and glowing like the Winnie the Pooh nightlight I'd outgrown just the previous year, the year Benny had been born.

A scratching noise caught my attention, woke me from the half-sleep I'd drifted into. I sat up in bed, looked out across the floor of my bedroom, scattered with toy cars and action figures, all lit stark with amber moonlight.

At first, I didn't see it. Then one of my action figures moved, and I realised I'd been looking straight at the fairy. My heart pounded as it approached. It looked more like an insect than a fairy, all long slim limbs with bulging joints. Its sharp fingers and toes scratched on the wooden floor like nails on a blackboard. Its head was almond-shaped, with large black eyes that shone liquid in the moonlight, colours running like an oil slick. When it blinked, the eyelids came from all sides at once, twin lenses irising in a split second. And its mouth was wide and thin, stretching half-way around its head like a snake's.

I'd imagined gossamer wings, but this fairy's wings belonged on a dead bat, flesh torn and rotting. At each wing's tip was a long, curved barb which scraped on the floor as the fairy dragged itself forward in a herky-jerky motion, grabbing at the floor, first one wing, then the other. But its eyes, its black, bottomless pits of eyes, they were always on me.

I remembered my dreams of a month ago. The crabs gnawing at my toes. Hungry. Hungry.

The fairy disappeared beneath the edge of my bed, and the scratching stopped. I wondered for a moment if I'd been dreaming, and now I was awake, alone in my room, no tiny skeletal monster scrabbling across the floor.

A barbed wing appeared at the end of my bed, hooking into my sheets. Then another. They pulled, and the fairy raised itself onto my bed and looked at me.

I didn't scream, barely breathed as it crawled towards me, still in that unreal stop-start manner. When it was almost upon me, it tilted its head to one side, quizzical.

Without taking my eyes off it, I reached under my pillow and pulled out the bone. I held it out, an offering.

It moved so fast I barely saw it. It snatched the bone from my hand with surprising strength, grasped it in its tiny needle-like fingers. It sniffed at it.

Then it opened its mouth.

Opened, and opened, and *opened*.

Its jaw unhinged, fell back against its emaciated body, and its whole head seemed to become a mouth. It jammed the bone into its maw. It kept going in, further than should have been physically possible, past the back of its head. Then the jaws snapped shut like a mousetrap. I heard a muffled crunch, watched the jaw grind as it chewed on the bone. It only took seconds, but it felt like forever, sitting there in my bed, no longer the safe place it had once been.

The fairy swallowed, blinked, then looked at me again. Those black eyes were dizzying, dangerous oily pools to drown in. Holding my eyes, the thing squatted on the bed and grunted. It straightened again, turned, and skittered away with shocking speed, gone from my bed in a heartbeat.

Left behind on my sheets was a lump of silver metal, white corrosion forming across its shiny surface, dulling it. I checked out my room, eyes darting from corner to corner, searching for the fairy.

There was no sign.

The room was empty, silent apart from my own ragged breathing and the fast thud-thud of my heartbeat in my ears. I fell back into my bed, the adrenaline fading from my veins. My eyelids were heavier than they'd ever been. Despite myself, despite what I'd seen, my eyes fell closed.

Then there was nothing. No dreams, no thoughts. Just nothing. Oblivion.

When I awoke the next morning, sunlight streaming through my window, I thought the whole awful thing had been a nightmare. But then I saw the metallic lump on my sheets, felt the absence of chicken bone beneath my pillow. Then I knew. It was real.

* * *

After that second time, I didn't want anything to do with the fairy again. I tried to tell my parents about it, but they thought I was just making up stories, trying to get their attention, jealous of Benny.

I wasn't, though. For the first time, I wasn't jealous of him. I just wanted my mummy and daddy to protect me from the horrible fairy.

I became withdrawn as the weeks passed, sullen. I didn't harass Cleo anymore, left the poor old thing alone. I was aware that, under her patchy fur and skin, she was made of bones. Everything was. Everyone was. My mum, my dad. Benny. All bones. Every time I looked at them, I saw the fairy, mouth impossibly wide.

Hungry.

Hungry.

My grades at school went down. Mum and Dad tried talking to me about it, but I didn't respond. How could I? I'd tried to tell them already. I felt like something inside me had broken, something that could never be fixed. How could they understand? They didn't believe me. I barely slept, awoken by any tiny noise, with my heart pounding. My appetite disappeared, replaced by a dull nausea that sat in the pit of my stomach.

"You have to eat," Mum said, face drawn with worry. "You're skin and bones."

I laughed at that, a bitter, hysterical laugh, and Mum recoiled, eyes terrified.

She wasn't afraid for me anymore. She was afraid of me.

The next full moon came, slowly waxing through the passing days until it shone bright and proud, almost a second sun in the dark, cloudless sky. That night I didn't sleep, *couldn't* sleep.

Don't worry. I haven't got any bones for the fairy, not tonight. The Tooth Fairy doesn't come if you don't put a tooth under your pillow. It's fine. It's fine.

But it wasn't fine. Not at all.

I didn't hear the fairy until it was on my bed. I'd left my bedroom door open to let the light from the corridor come in, somehow less scary than the moonlight that filled my room like pale honey, flooding it, drowning me in it. Then it was just *there*, on the edge, by my feet. My breath caught in my throat as it moved up the bed slowly, in those tiny sudden movements that haunted my nightmares. Made its way towards me.

There was a sudden flash of chocolate brown fur, and the fairy was gone, grabbed by Cleo who'd been hiding in my room again. She violently shook the creature in her mouth, growling deep in her throat.

She chomped once, twice, threw her head back, and swallowed the fairy.

It all happened so suddenly. Cleo looked at me with that disdainful satisfaction that cats all seemed to possess in spades, then sat back and started to wash herself. I just stared at her, shocked.

Cleo stopped washing herself. She coughed once, then again. Her green eyes found mine, and I saw something there that I'd never seen before, not in my whole life with her, through all our conflicts.

Fear.

She coughed again, but this time the sound caught half-way. Something was blocking her throat. She thrashed on the bed, clawing at everything in range, including my legs through the sheets. I reached out to her, tried to help, but she scratched at my hands. I pulled away; my fingers bloodied. Still, she struggled silently. Then, all at once, the fight went out of her and she collapsed onto her side, limp, her eyes wide open. Her mouth drooped open, pink tongue lolling out. Blood oozed onto my sheets.

A tiny hand emerged from the red wet darkness of Cleo's maw. The thin fingers closed around the bottom of the cat's jaw. Then another hand, this one grasping the top, slender fingers sliding between her bloodied fangs.

Nothing moved for a few seconds. Then, with a single violent motion, the hands pulled apart, and Cleo's furry face split in two, her jaws broken open. The hands pushed apart, and I could hear bones crack, flesh tear.

The fairy emerged from Cleo's mouth, covered in dark red blood. It clambered out of the dead cat's maw and studied me with those black eyes again. Then it turned and grabbed at the bottom of Cleo's jaw with both hands.

There was more cracking and tearing, and the fairy pulled the lower jawbone clear out of Cleo's head.

I screamed then, finally, screamed as the fairy ate the bone, screamed as it shat another lump of metal. Screamed as it scrambled away across my bed with preternatural speed. Screamed as it vanished.

I screamed as my parents turned my bedroom light on. I screamed as *they* screamed.

I thought I'd never stop screaming. In some ways, maybe I never have.

* * *

Psychologists. Tests. Therapists. More tests. The following weeks blurred together, muted by the cocktail of medications and treatments they tried on me. There was talk of me being committed, but my parents rejected that. I wonder sometimes if they regretted that decision later. I tried to tell them that I didn't kill Cleo, that it was the fairy, but they didn't believe me. How could they? They were grownups, and fairies were for children.

The weeks passed, and I pretended. I pretended I was all right, that everything was all right. Home life returned to…well, not normal, but bearable, at least. Mum was distracted by Benny, who was suffering from colic. Dad's work was frantic. They both focussed on other things, grateful not to be distracted by me anymore.

Once upon a time, that would have bothered me. Not anymore. I didn't want attention. I just wanted to be left alone. By Mum, by Dad.

And especially by the fairy.

There was no bone under my pillow, and it still came. I remembered Mum once told me never to give food to the magpie that lived in our jacaranda tree. *If you feed it, you'll never be rid of it.* I hadn't understood then, but I did now. I'd fed the fairy, and now I'd never be rid of it. It would come back again, and again, and again. Hungry. Hungry.

I had to kill it.

The next full moon came around terrifyingly quickly. A month used to be an eternity for me, as it was for every eight-year-old. Now I felt a hundred years older, my whole life measured in the wane and wax of the moon. That night, after my parents had gone to bed, I snuck downstairs to the kitchen, and grabbed a meat cleaver. I wasn't strong, but the cleaver was heavy, so I figured its weight would do most of the work for me. I'd seen my mum cut clean through an entire raw chicken once with that cleaver, with just a single blow.

I hid the cleaver underneath my pillow, same as the mouse skull, same as the chicken bone. This had all started underneath the pillow. Now it would end there, too.

I lay on my back, wide-awake, and listened as the hours passed. The room was full of moonlight. Nothing could hide. Not even a fairy.

It climbed onto the bed in one jerky motion. My heart was pounding, but not from fear, not this time. No, this time it was rage. I smiled as it approached, keeping its obsidian eyes on mine the whole way. It looked at me, head askew, mouth closed tight.

Hungry.

Hungry.

I nodded, reached under my pillow. My fingers found the hilt of the cleaver, wrapped around it as the fairy approached.

The instant it was in range, I whipped the cleaver out from beneath the pillow and swung it down at the fairy with all my strength.

There was a loud clang, and the cleaver just stopped. The impact jarred my shoulder, sending a lightning bolt of pain through my arm. The fairy had caught the cleaver with its wings, those fragile-looking, moth-eaten wings. Each barb hooked against the steel, holding it above the thing's slender head. Its eyes still on me.

It wrenched the cleaver from my weak hands, hurling it to the wooden floor. The blade spun over to the door, out of reach, useless.

The fairy's mouth opened, slowly, wider and wider as its jaws unhinged, like a ravenous anaconda preparing to swallow a bison.

I didn't scream, not this time. There was a sudden warmth in my pyjamas as I wet myself. I barely noticed. All I saw was the fairy. Its eyes. Its mouth.

A shrill sound drifted into the bedroom, distant but insistent. Benny was crying.

The fairy stopped, closed its mouth. Then it turned and moved away, so fast that it blurred. It scampered from the bed and across the bedroom floor. The thin wood of the door barely slowed its progress as it crunched straight through, taking one corner clean off.

I sat in bed, frozen. *He's your little brother,* my mum's voice echoed inside my head. *You have to protect him.* And she was right. He couldn't protect himself. I had to do it. I had to.

I didn't. I couldn't. I just sat there, pants soaked, clutching the sheets with paralysed hands. I sat, listening to Benny's crying. Listening, eyes closed tight, just listening.

His crying stopped, cut off.

I stayed there for a very long time, listening, praying for the cries to resume. To hear that horrible noise that I hated. I'd have given anything to hear it again. Anything.

I heard nothing. Terrible silence.

Eventually, I climbed out of bed, my pyjamas sodden. Near the door, my bare toes found the meat cleaver. I picked it up, then opened my door and looked down the hallway.

Benny's nursery door was open, just a crack. My parents had stopped closing it since Cleo had died. They didn't think there was any point anymore. They were wrong.

I crept down the hallway to the nursery door and listened. Nothing. No scratching, no crying. I pushed it open and stepped inside, looked at the cot.

Time slowed to a crawl. It was hard to breathe, or even to think, looking at… at that. At my little brother, who I was supposed to protect. At Benny.

At what was left of Benny.

The fairy had emptied him. There was nothing left but meat and skin, a crudely opened parcel of flesh, spread across the cot. So much blood for such a small body. How could there be so much blood? Benny was tiny. He was weak. He couldn't protect himself, not from Cleo, not from me. Certainly not from the fairy.

I was supposed to protect him.

Amongst the flesh, glistening like diamonds, were lumps of that silver-grey metal. Lots of them, hundreds, everywhere. So many.

I didn't scream, didn't cry. There was nothing left inside me to do either. Instead, I just curled up on the floor next to the cot, cradling the meat cleaver against my chest, and waited for dawn.

* * *

More doctors, more tests. This time I

was institutionalised. The police wanted to charge me with murder, but the doctors said I wasn't fit, even in juvenile court. That I wasn't mentally sound. I was put in the hospital, one of those hospitals where you're not allowed to leave, even if you want to.

I didn't care. I just waited. Waited for the next full moon, for the fairy to come for me.

But the full moon came and went, and the fairy didn't show. Another passed, and another. No fairy. The doctors told me that it was all in my head. They told me I'd killed Cleo, that I'd killed Benny. That I was very sick. They injected me with things that made me feel muffled inside, put electricity through my head.

Full moons smeared past me. No fairy. I was taking pills that made me sleep, but my dreams were filled with Benny and mantises Benny and crabs and Benny and… *oh my God Benny.*

Months became years. My parents visited at first, with kind words, but their faces told a different story. Their faces said that, when they looked at me, they saw Benny, not their beautiful baby boy, but the tattered mess left behind in the cot. They came less and less, and eventually stopped coming entirely.

Mum died in a car crash, apparently drunk. Soon after, my dad went to the beach and walked into the sea. They never found his body.

I was alone. Not even the fairy visited me.

Years and years, dozens of full moons. Beneath the weight of drugs and shocks and therapy, the fairy faded, became a nightmare, a fantasy. I *did* kill Cleo. And I *did* kill Benny. Fear became remorse.

The doctors said I was cured. They said I could leave the hospital. I was twenty-six years old.

It was hard, being in the real world. But I deserved it, deserved punishment. Got a job flipping burgers. A crappy apartment. Months passed, years. More full moons. No fairy.

Then I met Trish, and everything changed.

I never told her about my past. I couldn't. She'd have run away screaming. We were married two years after we met. I was thirty years old. A year later, she gave birth to our daughter, Alex. I felt complete, alive, for the first time in twenty-three years.

Twenty-three years. Or about three hundred lunar months. The number of bones in a baby, before a bunch of them join up, reducing the number. Three hundred, give or take.

* * *

Trish was a nurse and was working the night shift. I'd been left home with Alex. I was watching television when I heard something in our tiny two-bedroom apartment. I muted the television, the hairs on my arms and neck prickling. I glanced at the window and saw the moon.

The full moon.

Like a sleepwalker, I got to my feet and stumbled into the hall, to the single bedroom that was serving as Alex's nursery. Opened the door. Looked inside.

It was a dream. A fantasy. It didn't exist. I'd killed Cleo. I'd killed Benny.

Hadn't I?

The fairy perched on the head of my baby daughter's crib, its spindly body hunched, the claws of its wings gripping the rail tightly. Same black eyes blinking like camera lenses. It looked at me, then back to Alex.

Hungry. Hungry.

I screamed and lunged at it, grabbed the fairy with both hands. I fell to the floor and rolled on top of it, using my weight to pin it to the ground. I screamed again.

There was a sharp pain in my side, a stabbing, burning pain, and I cried out in agony, but I didn't let go. I couldn't. Not this time. Not again.

I didn't protect Benny. But I could protect Alex.

Something pushed against my body from beneath, and I was hurled aside with impossible force. My back slammed against the wall of the nursery. Stars sparkled in my vision. Distantly, Alex was crying now. I prayed that she'd keep crying. Keep crying, my baby girl. Keep crying.

She did.

My vision cleared. The fairy was standing on the floor beside me, looking into my eyes. It had something in its hands, grasped tight in its needle-like fingers. Something red and slick and curved.

It took longer than it should have to realise the fairy was holding a bone. A rib bone. *My rib bone.*

I looked down. My t-shirt had been sliced open. My flesh was sliced, too. There was a lot of blood. My head swam. I didn't like blood, didn't like pain. Just like when I was eight and a half.

The fairy opened its awful mouth wide and ate my rib. Then it crouched and took a shit of soft metal on my daughter's nursery floor, before turning and speeding from the room.

I lay there, bleeding but relieved, so relieved. I hadn't protected Benny, but I'd protected my baby daughter. I'd protected Alex.

My relief dried up, turned to dread. This time. I'd protected her this time.

I clambered to my feet, shaky and sweating and nauseated. I looked down at my daughter, at the most precious thing I could ever imagine. Just took her in, while she cried fiercely. *Keep crying.* A sad smile twisted my lips awkwardly. *Keep crying. It means you're alive. It means I protected you.*

I bent and kissed her on the head for the last time, then turned and left the apartment, her frightened screams filling my senses long after the sound was gone.

* * *

That was five years ago. Or was it six? I've lost count.

I live on the streets, alone. It's safer that way. Nobody else gets hurt. I don't want anyone else getting hurt, never again. This is my problem, mine alone.

Alone. It's best. One mistake, and you're damned.

It's a full moon again, and I'm waiting, huddled in a cardboard box under a bridge. I've travelled clear across the country, trying to outrun the fairy, but I can't, I know that, even if I could still run. It's a full moon, and it'll come for me, as it does every full moon.

Feed it once and you'll never get rid of it. Hungry. Hungry.

I tried to fool it, after I lost my rib and my life in the same night. The next full moon after that, I waited with a goodly variety of animal bones I'd taken from rubbish bins, stored up and hoarded, waiting. Hoping. The fairy went straight past them and took the end clean off my left index finger in a single bite. I even tried human bones, dug up from a little graveyard in the suburbs, but it didn't want them. I knew that, even before I tried. It didn't want them.

It wanted me.

What's left of my body. So many bones taken. My whole right leg, most of my left. The toes slowed it down, so many little bones there. Same with my hands. I still have one finger and a thumb remaining on my left hand. My right arm is gone. About half my ribs have been taken, and the bones inside both my ears, leaving me deaf. I don't mind that, really. It stops me hearing that awful skittering as its nails and wing barbs scrape on the ground.

There, to my left, the shadows of the full moon shift. It's coming. I close my eyes and wait, accustomed to the pain and blood now. It doesn't bother me anymore. Because as long as it's me, my pain, my blood, then Alex is safe. I've protected her. Maybe that'll make up for Benny.

There are two hundred and six bones in the adult body. I wonder how many more the fairy can take before it kills me.

THE REAPING
BY JAY CASELBERG

He lies there in the field
Down by the south fence
Among the long grass
Belly waxing gibbous
His eyes stare skyward
Now milky
His face expressionless
It gives no clue
No pain
No sorrow
Just blankness

One by one
He drove them all away
With arrogance and bluster
And his insecurity
There are none to find him now
Except for wildlife
And perhaps the birds
A feast

CARBON COPY CONSUMABLES
BY DEBORAH SHELDON

Look, what you've got to understand about industry—and I'm talking about the food industry in particular—is that the pursuit of money always trumps common sense. It's been this way since Year Dot. For instance, there's only one type of banana for sale across the whole planet, the Cavendish, but here's the kicker: each piece of fruit is a clone. I'm not bullshitting you. They're grown from suckers. So, every banana is genetically identical. If a pathogen comes along that can wipe out just one banana, it'll wipe out the crop worldwide.

And this isn't a theory, mind you. It happened already.

Prior to the Cavendish, the only commercial banana was another cloned variety, the Gros Michel, and that crop got destroyed by a kind of soil fungus in the 1960s. The Cavendish was its replacement. But did the food industry learn anything from putting all its eggs—or Gros Michel bananas—into the one basket? No, except to do it all over again because of economics. Even when the smallest possible risk is complete and utter catastrophe. You see where I'm coming from? Money trumps common sense. Every. Single. Time.

Don't get me wrong, I'm not against food cloning. That's my trade, after all. Cloning is a great idea. Finding a way to computerise, mechanise, and standardise the process solved a lot of problems like overfishing, deforestation, famines, and suchlike and et cetera, but hey, I don't need to make a speech. Anybody with half a brain knows that food cloning factories are a boon to mankind. I'm only stating my point of view for the record.

Also, for the record, my name is Charles Pomeroy, but everyone calls me Charlie. I'm thirty-four years old, single, no kids, Aussie by birth, and a factory runner for Carbon Copy Consumables. For the past eight years, I've worked at their Antarctica plant servicing the research stations, hotels, resorts, casinos, theme park, restaurants, private homes and what have you. The busiest time of year is summer when the tourist ships come by the dozen and every business is running at full capacity. With about nine thousand mouths to feed, I have to run the factory twenty-four seven. Yeah, all by my lonesome.

The company website explains their setup if you're interested, but in a nutshell, the Antarctica factory is about a kilometre long, three storeys high, covered in gantries and stuffed to the gills with machines. Carbon Copy Consumables is 'lights-out' manufacturing with everything controlled by a bunch of computers. Even the trucks that pick up the supplies are automated and self-driven, and each truck is packed by robot arms.

So, the four reasons I'm needed there…

One: feed the machines. Our base material looks like bouillon powder. It's actually a combination of elements including carbon, nitrogen, sulphur—I forget the others—but ninety-seven percent of every living thing on Earth is made up of just six elements. Amazing, right? At full storage capacity, I've got six vats and each one's about the size of a wheat silo.

Two: keep the joint hygienic. The machines have self-cleaning cycles; I top up detergents.

Three: equipment maintenance. Our machines are so smart they're almost self-sufficient, the emphasis on 'almost'. Nothing beats the human mind. Training to be a factory runner takes four years because you need to learn how to service every part of every machine. Yeah, there's manuals to jog your memory, but it's a specialised field with lifelong job security. Why would Carbon Copy Consumables sack a factory runner after investing four years into them? And you get paid top dollar while you train. Sweet gig. If you ever want a career change, look into it. Just be aware the competition is stiff. For every opening, there's a thousand applications. You've got to be the best of the best.

And four: stock control. The machines can't make informed decisions about which foods need to be cloned. I take orders from all over Antarctica. You've got no idea of the vast amount of produce I churn out to allow three meals and snacks for nine thousand people in peak season. Hold onto your little cotton socks because I'm about to blow your mind. Ready?

Five tonnes of vegetables. That's metric tonnes, mind you, per day. Two tonnes of beef, every cut from chuck to eye fillet. One tonne of chicken. Ten thousand eggs. All. Per. Day. And so on, and so forth. Can you grasp the scale of this operation? Can you imagine trying to fly this amount of naturally-sourced food into Antarctica? Well, that's how they used to do it in the old days. That's why the population was capped at about one thousand; the logistics of supply were too difficult.

Oh yeah, and another reason: a bunch of Antarctic Treaties about keeping the continent pristine. Those treaties were overturned for the sake of money. Capitalism is great, don't get me wrong—it's

dragged most of the world out of poverty— but there's a few drawbacks here. Did you know that one-third of Antarctica is now a giant tip covered in garbage? Anyhow, that's progress. Two steps forward, one step back. Don't worry, a company will come up with a way to turn rubbish into something useful, like gold, if there's money in it.

Sure, I'm on good terms with the freight runners, ship captains, pilots, et cetera. You know what? Cards on the table? I'll come straight out and tell you that my partner in the botany scheme was a pilot named Jenny. I'm guessing you're interrogating her anyway, so there's no point me trying to be discreet. The whole sideline about the plants was her idea, with a forty-sixty split. She promised me bucketloads of cash, and boy, was she right on the money.

There are two flowering plants native to Antarctica: the hair grass and the pearlwort. You find them mainly on the western peninsula and on a couple of islands. Jenny told me this one time, while she was waiting on her plane to be refuelled and loaded, that some knob-ends from Sydney's North Shore were scouting for unusual plants for their daughter's bridal bouquet and table arrangements, and would I be interested in some quick dough?

Now, these Antarctic plants look pretty dull, but that's not the point. Rarity symbolises wealth. Even if the plants happened to look like busted arseholes covered in fly-blown crap, it wouldn't matter. Do you know what happened in the seventeenth century when the pineapple was first brought over to Britain from Barbados? Well, the pineapple was such a rare fruit, and so expensive, that super-rich people would bung one in the middle of their ballroom and host a party to flex on their high-society friends. The not-so-rich rented pineapples for the sole purpose of bragging. Even a rotting pineapple had prestige.

And hundreds of years later, rich people are exactly the same.

Long story short, yeah, I cloned the plants, and Jenny sold them to this family. Within months, Jenny and me had an enterprise. Strictly under the table, of course. It's not like we took out ads. Word of mouth only. Just like the trade in stolen art works, right? Inner circle stuff. People want to show off to their mates, not get arrested by Interpol.

Oh, we made money for jam. And we never worried about us double-crossing each other. Jenny couldn't run the plants through the machines herself because cloning is locked down tighter than the diamond industry. I couldn't get plants out of Antarctica without a pilot's licence, and besides that, didn't have any contacts with buyers. Jenny and I were partners in crime. Both of us faced jail. We had reasons to be faithful to our handshake.

But word gets around in the upper echelons of the filthy rich.

And soon, Jenny came to me with another request, this time from Asia. Some billionaire wanted to throw a dinner party with penguin on the menu.

Look, I'm not going to debate which animals are okay to eat and which ones aren't. As far as I'm concerned, once you've eaten meat, you've crossed a line and can't wag the finger at anybody for their choices. Still, I had to think about this offer for a long, long while. Could I really offer up cloned penguins knowing they were destined for someone's cooking pot?

Jenny had convincing arguments, namely… I provided beef, lamb, pork, and chicken as food, didn't I, so what's the difference? The penguin destined for the table wouldn't be the original or 'real' penguin, just a clone, while the real penguin would be released back into the wild, unharmed, free to live its life, swim and raise babies. Penguins get eaten by seals and orcas every day, so why not by people? Et cetera. Bottom line: the money was jaw-dropping.

Antarctica has lots of different penguins like king, adélie, chinstrap, gentoo. Penguins are fast in water; on land they're bumbling idiots. My first penguin was a chinstrap, so-called because it has this little banding of black feathers under its beak. It's an aggro species but small and real clumsy on the ice. It took five minutes to stuff one in my backpack. Hey, there's about eight million of the buggers; it wasn't like taking one for a couple of hours would upset the balance of anything important.

Right?

And yet…I'd never put a live animal through the machines. For some reason, I imagined the cloned penguin would be turned inside-out. Crazy, huh? I had to keep reminding myself that fruit and vegies are alive when they're cloned. Oh yes, of course they are—if they were dead, they'd be withered and black.

Even so, I had a big problem. The machines can't read anything that's moving because they work on similar principles to 3D food printers. I had to find a way to keep the penguin as still as possible. I chose sleeping pills. My working hours are all over the place. Naturally, I've got stashes. I figured the medication would stay in the bird's guts and blood, and not migrate into its muscles. Therefore, anyone who ate its meat wouldn't get dosed.

I cloned the drugged bird.

The process takes seventeen minutes for the first replication. After that, once the sequencing is worked out, the replication rate is lightning fast: pow, pow, pow. The cloned penguins were asleep, which made packaging and transportation much easier. Since we use automated systems to load trucks and planes, only me and Jenny knew what was going on.

Good God, over the next year…

Money, money, money.

So much money…

Occasionally, there were 'exposés' on blogs and threads about illegal penguin meat, but the mainstream media figured it was an urban myth. Hah! I supplied every kind of penguin that exists in Antarctica. Yet each specimen I kidnapped was returned, unharmed, to the ice shelf where I found it. I never penned any of them to save time. That would've been cruel. And remember, the clones exported for eating purposes weren't 'real' in the same way the original penguins were real. Manufactured clones don't count. That's law, right?

Soon we got other requests. Antarctic seabirds became popular: blue-eyed shag, giant petrel, snowy sheathbill, cape pigeon. But these birds can fly! Trapping them required ingenuity on my part; luckily, I'm very intelligent. The price per kilo had to be higher than for penguins. Astronomically higher. That said, Antarctic seabirds are stringy. You've got to braise them low and slow. Even if you're a pro chef who does everything perfectly, the meat still comes out dry, chaffy, tasteless. Look, it's not about flavour. Remember the pineapple? If dog shit was rare, the one-percenters would serve it at dinner parties with silver spoons.

Did I eat any of these meats? No. Beef, chicken, lamb, pork: that'll do fine. Occasionally I eat fish and seafood, but don't come at me with weird shit like eel, oysters, or sea urchin. Novelty doesn't interest me. I won't try a food just for the 'experience'. Not that I'm shaming anyone who's into that kind of thing. Live and let live, I always say.

So, dealing in cloned plants, penguins, seabirds…as you can imagine, I was busy.

Busy enough that I swapped sleeping pills for amphetamines. The factory ran twenty-four seven and I had a side business that was essentially a full-time job in itself—when could I sleep? And the money was another time-sink. Do you know how difficult it is to launder and hide cash? You can't use bank accounts without explaining why, how, when, and the tax department always sticks in its beak. From necessity, I stayed awake for three, sometimes four days at a stretch. Ah, crazy times… But after a few years, I was going to retire and cruise the world on a five-hundred-foot yacht.

It was exhaustion, I guess. Desperation. Amphetamines don't create energy; they stop you from sleeping, and the sleep debt adds up. Then you start making dumb decisions. That's the only way I can explain it. One day, when I was popping another pill and staring in the mirror at the black bags under my eyes, I thought, "Why the hell am I killing myself, burning the candle at both ends—and in the middle too—when there's such an easy solution?"

Sure, the idea gave me pause. Each of us likes to think of ourselves as unique. But I got to pondering about identical twins, triplets, quadruplets, quintuplets. I'm an only child. Would it be so bad to have a 'brother'? We could split the chores. Perhaps share some of my money. I was the mastermind, so any divvying of funds would be at my discretion since the clone would be my employee, right? I know how it sounds, but it made perfect sense at the time.

Putting myself into the machine was like taking a seat in an untested rollercoaster. You're doing something that should be perfectly safe, at least in theory, but feels terrifying. The machine clicked, hummed, buzzed, whirred, knocked, whistled, tapped, and each sound scared the absolute shit out of me as I lay on the table, motionless, because I'd never heard those sounds before and I began to panic, wondering if something had gone wrong, if I would die. Get turned inside-out.

Let me tell you, that was an excruciating seventeen-minute wait.

The alarm went off: the sequencing and first replication had finished. I laughed and cried in relief. I'd only keyed in one clone. Just one. I got off the table and ran to the other end of the factory, which took about five minutes. The Other Charlie was standing there in my uniform. You know what surprised me? It turns out I'm bow-legged. I had no idea. The other thing that bothered me was his posture. His shoulders were tilted one way and his hips the other, as if there was a sideways bend in his spine, but subtle, very mild. I guess I was critical because I was seeing myself in the flesh for the first time. I looked old. Maybe that was on account of how tired I was, so empty and rundown.

"Charlie?" I said. "Do you understand what's going on?"

"Perfectly," he said. "Let's get started."

"Sweet," I said. "Run the shift while I get some shut-eye. I'll be back later with a chinstrap penguin."

"No worries," he said, and went about his—our—business.

I had the most restful sleep I've enjoyed in ages. Then I took a snowmobile and headed to an ice shelf. Have you ever visited Antarctica? It's beautiful. Light-blue ice

mountains, clear sky, snow in all shades and textures. Anyway, I spotted a crowd of chinstrap penguins—they stick out like dog's balls against the white landscape—and parked my snowmobile about half a kilometre distant, so the engine noise wouldn't spook them. I walked the rest of the way. And as I trudged over the last little rise, damned if I didn't find the Other Charlie squatting there, wrestling a penguin into his backpack while a horde of angry penguins shrieked at him.

"What the hell's going on?" I said, pissed off. "Why aren't you at the factory?"

"What are you talking about?" he said. "You're the one supposed to be running the shift."

"Bullshit," I said. "So, who's running the shift?"

"I guess nobody is now," he said, and looked annoyed, pouting, as if I was the one who'd done the wrong thing. "We'd better get back. I've got a penguin already, so let's go."

We rode to town on our respective snowmobiles. I was fuming the whole journey. Clearly, the Other Charlie was throwing his weight around. He wanted to be equal partners, not my employee. But as the original Charlie Pomeroy, I had first dibs. As we neared civilisation, I wracked my brains, trying to figure how to rein in this cheeky bastard.

Back at the factory, we both got a surprise.

Some Other Charlie was there and he looked just as shocked to see us.

"How come there's two of you?" he said. "What the hell's going on?"

"You're asking *me* what's going on?" I said. "I'm the one who deserves answers."

"Why do *you* deserve answers?" the Other Charlie said, hands on hips.

The three of us got to arguing. My theory:

Other Charlie had the same bright idea and had cloned himself while I'd slept. However, Other Charlie and Some Other Charlie were both now insisting they were the original, which was ludicrous, considering it was me who first went through the replication process. Meanwhile, the penguin thrashed inside the backpack, squawking its head off, and I started to worry the little bugger was going to hurt himself. When the three of us headed to the backpack at the same time, we halted, stunned.

"What the hell's going on?" said a voice, and blow me if there wasn't a fourth Charlie walking over, his face pale and shocked. "How come there's three of you?"

And the four of us yelled at the same time, "What the hell's going on?", which made the hairs stand up on the back of my neck. But it scared my clones in the exact same way and when I saw the identical expressions of fear on their faces, I started to shake. They started shaking too in perfect mimicry. I was caught in a hall of mirrors. My heart banged hard enough to explode. Meanwhile, the trapped penguin screeched over and over. We turned to the backpack as one. And then—

"What the hell's going on?" said a voice.

Christ, it was another Charlie. I can't explain the horror!

Then another Charlie appeared. And another...and another...

God, the way I figure it, each clone must have cloned himself, unaware.

After some fraught arguing, the bunch and I ended up cooperating to scour the kilometre of factory from one end to the other in order to flush out any other Charlies. Meanwhile, more Charlies kept arriving at intervals with kidnapped penguins. Each time, we'd have to stop and have another pow-wow.

God, if it wasn't so terrifying, maybe it'd be funny.

We walked together in a line, shoulder to shoulder. Each of us ignored the distressed penguins without discussion. We found about a dozen more Charlies at various points, who joined our search, while others kept coming in from outside, bearing penguins. The birds wouldn't stop calling to each other, distressed and frantic. The chinstrap sounds a lot like a seagull, did you know that? I kept closing my eyes against their cries, trying to imagine that I was on a beach somewhere and only dreaming this nightmare, until I noticed my clones doing the same thing and felt a heart-seizing panic attack coming on.

When the alarm sounded, we froze and stared at each other in terror. The alarm meant that yet another Charlie had been created, and would soon be jogging towards us from the far end of the factory, shouting, "What the hell's going on?" I'd forgotten to turn off the machines. We all had. How many clones in total? Oh God, I don't know. I couldn't even guess...

Getting sprung by the authorities was my fault.

Whenever I cloned a plant, penguin or seabird, I deleted the history from the logs. For some reason—probably because I was sleep-deprived—I forgot to do that after making the Other Charlie. And because he's me, he forgot to delete the history when he created his own clone, and so on. That tripped a red flag at Carbon Copy Consumables, and then military police came, and well...you know the rest.

Listen, I understand that clones aren't protected under any laws or Geneva conventions. Fair enough. Unauthorised clones have to be put down. No complaint from me on that score. My only issue is that you destroy the clones and not me by mistake. I'm happy to go to jail if that's my punishment, or pay a fine or whatever. Surely, there's some way to tell us apart? A medical test. Isn't there? There has to be. The clones might be telling you the exact same story, but my statement is the truth, I swear to God, because I'm the real deal. Okay? Hand on heart. I am the original Charlie Pomeroy.

BRUMATION
BY ANTHONY FERGUSON

I always like to tell folks it was the weather that brought me across state lines to Texas, but that ain't really so. Nor was it the gators, even though catching and skinning 'em was my line of work for a piece.

Not a lot of people know that gators get as far west as Texas. But yessir, state lines don't mean a damn to them. Long as they got agreeable water, they'll get all the way from Florida through Louisiana and into oil country.

Truth is, it was Willie Nixon that dragged me west. Even if I didn't have proof of his true nature at the time, I came trotting along on account of him, and them things he done. Real awful inhuman stuff. Like some kind of beast rather than a man.

I say this as one who knew folks got caught up in the Indian wars and seen some of the atrocities them savages committed. Cutting up folk and taking scalps and sometimes whole heads and putting 'em on display. Christ, even cutting off the lower regions as well. Then there was what they did to white women.

I heard sure as night follows day that some settlers got to leaving their last round of bullets to put into the heads of their women and children, rather than let the Injuns get at 'em. Then again, I also heard talk of some of the stuff the whites did to the Indians too, and that was just as bad. Raping and butchering their women and children, burning their villages and such like. Pure horrible stuff, and I was a mite grateful that the Indian wars were about done by the time I headed west, back in '88.

It goes without saying them days were hard, and a lot of people did a lot of suffering. I know that well enough on account of what Nixon did to my sweetheart, Annabelle, but I see I'm getting ahead of myself. So I'll start at the beginning.

* * *

As a young man, I set out working on whaling ships out of Nantucket. A fine sort of life for a lad, adventuring on the high seas with a bunch of rowdy coves. Made a man out of me. But comes a time when a man wants to settle and start a family, like I wanted with Annabelle.

While I don't wish to dwell too long on my love, on account of how she ended up and all, it's important for you to know that she came from out west. Put herself out a lot for me, good woman that she was, but we both came to agree that it ain't no good for a marriage to have the feller away at sea for months on end, especially on journeys which he may not return from, as many didn't. God rest their souls.

So it turned out there weren't that many jobs around for a feller skilled with a knife. Least, not the kind of work that paid enough to set up a home for a wife with a baby on the way.

That's how come I took to the gator skinning game. Plus, the sallying forth by boat made it so I didn't miss the high seas and ships too much. Even better, none of the gator trapping trips lasted more than a day or two, week at the most, and only in the high season.

Gatoring is hard work, mind, and like whaling, you get paid by the amount of beasts you catch and skin. I sank most of my savings into my first boat, a real little beauty.

Can't catch gators alone. Well, you can, but it's a mite easier with a buddy. Gotta have one feller to navigate, the other to haul up the traps. Both have to be good and quick with the knife once you drag the critter on board.

Had me a good partner in ol' Solly Marsh. Stayed with me a good two years afore that gator took off most the fingers on his right hand—the skinning hand.

I was sorry to see Solly go, but I done him right with money and all. I made damn sure of that. Matter of fact, it was down near Solly's old place the first bodies showed up. First ones we knew of, anyway. Found 'em floating downstream in the river, caught up in the bulrushes. What was left of 'em.

Sure, the gators had been at them, but it weren't that which made us swallow hard and cuss. It was the ropes tied around the wrists, and the obvious signs that someone had been at them with a knife. Solly had to usher his kids away, hollering at them not to look backwards.

They was women both, except that someone had taken to cutting out their private bits, their titties too. Punctured 'em fulla holes and even took out their eyes.

"God almighty," I recall saying to Solly at the time. "Damn gators didn't do all this."

It didn't make a lick of sense, Solly agreed, why anyone would do this to a body, no matter how much they felt they'd been wronged. I knew of men who had offed their wives for running around with other fellers, but this…this was beyond what any man would do. This was monstrous.

Well, we reported it, naturally, and the sheriff took up the case. Two women, unrelated. Though it musta been hard to tell from the state of them. They blamed the Indians of course. We let it go at that.

I had other stuff on my plate round the time, like finding me a new offsider. That's how I met Willie. He was just a few years older than me. A real man's man. Had spent much of his youth out west serving in the US cavalry, as he told it. Matter of fact, he reminded me of pictures I'd seen of Custer, with his flowing golden locks, bushy moustache, and bright blue eyes. Willie sure turned the ladies' heads.

It surprised me that he weren't hitched himself, till he told me that he lost his sweetheart to the savages. Damn near made me lose my dinner when he described what they did to her, cutting her up something awful after they'd had their way with her.

The way he described it brought up images of them two bodies in the river, so I told him about that. Then I near choked again when he let on there had been others. More bodies turning up in rivers, in several towns along the state line.

When I called him out, he pulled from his rucksack some clippings from the papers about the killings. Said he kept them on account of what happened to his girl. That he hoped to catch them at it one day. Then he slipped a big Bowie knife out of his boot and espoused on what he would do to them when he caught them.

"Rogue Indians for sure," he said. "No civilised man would behave in this manner."

I had him read some of the accounts out loud to me, seeing as I never did learn to read too good, having left home to go to sea at the age of twelve. But Willie had gotten himself a decent education.

Seemed a mite odd to me he didn't have no steady woman either. Given every time we stopped off somewhere for a bite or a libation, the young ladies would gravitate toward him. They ignored me of course, on account of my ornery looks and my wedding band, but Willie had him a way with words and a certain charm about him the ladies found appealing. Like bees around a honey pot. I even felt a pang of jealousy. Was almost tempted not to take him home and introduce him to Annabelle. Did though. Damn my sorry hide. He was sweet as pie, though, and treated her like royalty. I swear she was even sweet on him too, though she insisted otherwise.

More important was how good Willie was at his work. Wasn't long afore we was bringing in near twice what poor Solly and me used to do, and I was suckered in by all that money that would be so handy for my impending family. Willie was a breeze to work with. Always whistling and smiling, and I've never seen anybody handle a knife like that man. Had that gator out of its skin quicker than a whore out of her britches on payday.

I paint this picture so as to illustrate I never had no inkling as to Willie Nixon's true nature. That wouldn't come out till way later, and by that point, it was too late for me. No, it was like Willie was wearing a second skin of his own. One that somehow disguised his real face. That's what Deputy Briggs would say to me after, or words to that effect.

Suffice to say that them women's bodies kept popping up. Not in a flood, mind, but a steady flow. Always along the rivers and creeks. All of 'em desecrated in a similar manner too. With eyeballs, teeth, hands, and sometimes the whole heads removed. Sometimes the monsters even cut out their hearts.

Not that I ever saw any of it, thank the Lord. What I seen out back of Solly's was bad enough. But Willie took a keen interest in the matter and would regale me with lurid tales from the press cuttings he'd acquired.

The law was still running around in the dark on the killings, and it didn't matter how many stray Injuns, or negroes, or gunslingers they strung up, them bodies kept on piling up. They even questioned poor old Sol and asked to look at his knives, but I knew damn well my old pal had nothing to do with it.

I should stress that policing weren't too flash in them days, and if a killer managed to cross state lines, well, that sheriff there had to cede to the next one along, and so on. It was like the killer or killers knew this and was deliberately sowing confusion to terrorise the decent law-abiding folks. It worked.

That's how I come to that day… I don't want to dwell on the details none. God knows I talked enough about it in the weeks and months after. My Annabelle was only just startin' to show, and it pained me to think the savages knew it when they cut her.

I was screaming by the time they dragged me away from her. I just wanted to hold my Belle one more time, even if it woulda been hard to do on account of what state she was in, but the wedding ring still attached to her hand, that did me in.

Willie was good enough to keep the boat running for me till I got back on board 'bout a month later. After the burial. Saw him too at the graveyard, but he kept a distance, just giving me a pat on the shoulder in passing.

Told me how sorry he was when we finally headed back out on the river. Vowed again to get his hands on the killers. I just nodded without speaking and he backed away. He knew it was still a mite raw for me.

Now this next bit is almost as hard to tell and near as awful as what happened to my kin. Thing is, I knew the details of the savagery perpetrated on my bride, and I don't know if Willie knew that, or knew enough of it.

Anyways, we was drinking in a bar after another good day of kills on the river. I was drowning my sorrows as it were, and Willie was doing his best to help me.

At some point, he took out a coin purse to pay for a round and I happened to notice the skin of it. Sort of a weird colour and texture. I asked him if it was gator, and when I reached out to touch it, he pulled it away.

Willie said it was from a boar he took down, but it was the way he said it that got at me. The look in his eyes was wrong, like it weren't him there at all, but someone else underneath. Best way I can say it. Twas then I really paid attention to the chain hanging around his neck. He hadn't had that piece when I first took him on, and I strained to recall when it first appeared on his person.

Now I did all this on account of two things. One being something the mortician let slip to me at the station. That the killer or killers were taking stuff from the victims. Sometimes body parts, other times accoutrements. Sometimes both.

Two. The sons of bitches had skinned my Annabelle's arm.

I didn't press him, but it occurred to me that Willie didn't want none of me touching his pouch. Whipped it away out sight real quick. I got to thinking why he would do that if it was just some old boar he'd taken the hide off. After all, he'd let me try on his gator skin boots not a month earlier.

I shoulda gone straight to the sheriff's office with my suspicions, but I didn't. Just sat there like a dunderhead, mulling it over in disbelief. Worse still, I let Willie see the look in my eye.

That night, I paced around in my now empty shack, a whiskey bottle on the table before me. I'd already downed one glass when it occurred to me how vulnerable I might be. Even me, a big strong feller in the prime of life.

Don't for the life of me know what made me hit the deck at that very moment. I turned toward the open window, strong breeze blowing the curtains Anabelle had picked out at the store before she…

Maybe I saw the muzzle flash; I don't know. But I hit the deck and the bullet crashed into the wall opposite.

I grabbed my rifle and ran out into the dark, hollering. Damn fool thing to do, but maybe I hoped to scare him by it. As it was, there was no more shots. Whoever it was had hightailed it away into the woods.

Willie never showed up at the boat next day. In fact, he never showed up again. I reported it all to the sheriff, and they put out an account. But of Willie Nixon there was neither sight nor sound. Sheriff Polsen told me that Willie had no doubt crossed the state line and not to trouble myself. A telegraph had gone out for all parties to keep an eye out for the suspect, set with a good photographical picture, too. I say suspect because the law was still fixing to blame the whole mess on the Injuns. No white man could have committed these sins, was the general consensus of God-fearing folk.

But I knew what I knew, and I wasn't about to let it rest.

Another thing ol' Willie didn't know about me was that I'm an expert tracker of beast or man. Just got an affinity for it. Learned much of it at my daddy's side as a boy.

So whether he knew it or not, I had Willie's scent, and I was on his trail. I knew too that he would give me a sign, sooner or later. One way or another.

That sign came when I was drowning my

sorrows one night in a tavern. I overheard a group of woodsmen talking excitedly. Another body had been found in the shallows of a river out west of Louisiana. This one at a place not far from Houston. This one feller was jabbing at the air, indicating the state of the body, and how and where she had been cut, dissected as it were. Sure, the body was gator bit, but there was no denying the other handiwork had been done by human hand.

I swear this cove's eyes was fit to bust out of his head as he described how the poor girl had been carved. Straight away, I knew it was Nixon's handiwork. It was as if he were calling to me. I quietly drained my tankard, walked home to my dead empty house, and started fixing to sell up and put all my worldly goods in store.

That's when I headed west, on the trail of new hunting grounds, following the water, looking for gators, and another type of monster too.

On my travels, I reflected on some of the tales Nixon had regaled me with around the campfire, his eyes all shining with what I now figured to be excitement. He would ponder as to just how the killer had subdued and cut up them poor gals, carefully selecting which pieces of flesh to carve out. How he stuck his hands inside their guts and pulled out their innards. How he musta got some kind of sick pleasure out of tampering with them like that.

Now I damn near choked thinking on all that stuff, on account of what the sheriff told me about my dear departed wife, how they'd found the killer's seed on her. Then I thought deep about Nixon and gripped the handle of my gator knife real tight, thinking on what I was fixing to do when I caught up with him.

Well, I made sure my appearance on the gator hunting scene was well publicised round that part of Texas. Advertised for an offsider, even though I had no intention of taking one, unless it was the one I was after. I set out my traps in more ways than one, now I just needed him to take the bait.

The next sign he gave of his presence came floating on the tide past my boat one morning in late summer. More than three months since we parted ways. The decomposing torso of another young woman, minus the eyes, all of its limbs, and a hole where her heart shoulda been.

I figured he cut out the eyes because he didn't want them looking at him while he worked at them, carrying out his vile acts of cruelty.

It did occur to me that I had a moral obligation to bring the law into it, and how it might save the lives of more unfortunate women, but to my shame I was now Hell bent on revenge. Too filled with bitter hatred to let anyone get their hands on the murderer but me.

Late summer marked the end of gator season. As the leaves turned to brown and the waters grew colder, an idea fixed itself in my brain.

I knew Nixon wasn't a true gator man. Soon as the weather turned, he always lit out for warmer climes. Taking himself anywhere he could practise his true calling, with the knife. This time, I knew he would stick around because of me, but I would be ready.

I set up home in an old shack not far from the river's edge, and sat and waited for the snows to come. I knew he would come for me soon enough.

Took to sitting out on the porch in full view, braving the cold, wrapped up tight in blankets. Shotgun on my lap. It was a risk, but one I had to take.

Late one afternoon, as I was starting to doze despite the cold, a voice hailed me from the edge of the woods.

"Mite cold to be sittin' out ain't it?"

My eyes eased open to pinpoint the voice, while my fingers slid around the barrel of my shooter. Then I fixed on the figure skulking under the trees, dressed in furs. The golden curls were gone, his head shaved bare. The moustache too, but the piercing blue eyes still glittered with hidden knowledge.

"That you out there, Willie Nixon?" I asked, showing him my hand.

He stepped forward into the light, the wind whipping around his collar. He held his own rifle out before him.

"Been a long time, Zeke. Too long. I know you got me figured. Thought we could sort this, man to man."

He edged closer. I sat upright. Both of us pointing our weapons.

"Why d'ya do it, Willie? Why d'ya take my woman?"

He shook his head. "I'm damn sorry, Zeke. I just can't control it. The fever comes over me, and I just gotta cut 'em. See what's inside them beautiful critters." He looked down at his rifle. "Even these things don't do it for me. Makes it too impersonal, if you understand."

"How comes you tried to shoot me through my window back east then? I figure that was you."

"I fired over your head, Zeke. That's why you're still sittin' there."

When I thought back to it, I recalled how high the bullet went into the wall. Nixon weren't lying to me.

"Well, if you ain't fixing to shoot me then, what do you want, Willie?"

He lowered his gun. "Well sir, it occurs to me you tailed me out here for a reason.

It's you that wants dealin' with me, not the other way round."

"True." I lowered my own gun slightly.

"So, how's about we do it man to man? My blade against your blade. Like true gator men."

As I watched him, Nixon laid his gun in the snow, and slowly drew his knife from his boot.

"Whadya say, Zeke?"

I laid my gun at my feet and rose slowly.

"If that's the way you want it, Willie. Find me fair."

I drew my own blade and stepped off the porch. Took a couple of steps toward him and stopped. I tried my damndest to keep my eyes on his, and not on the ground between us.

He frowned. "You fixin' to trick me somehow, Zeke?"

"No, I'm fixing to cut you, Willie. She was with child, you know."

"I know, Zeke…but I weren't sure whose it were…yours or mine." A sly grin lit his face, and I screamed and charged at him.

"You son of a bitch!"

Willie forgot his hesitation and came at me, the blade held afore him. I stopped in the nick of time, praying that I hadn't miscounted my steps under that day's fall of snow.

Nixon got within a couple of feet when I heard the sharp snap of the bear trap clamping around his foot. He let out a piercing scream and lurched forward. I swept my blade across his fingers, severing the front three at the knuckle and sending the knife spinning out of his grip. Blood sprang from the bloody stumps and soiled the white earth.

Recoiling in shock, Nixon sat down hard on the seat of his pants. His good hand flew to the steel jaws of the trap, and he let out a series of involuntary moans.

I stood and regaled him a good few minutes till he calmed down, then I went for him. Nixon raised his good hand to protect his face and I hacked that son-of-a-bitch clean off. He screamed again and fell back into a dead faint.

I picked up the unconscious body and carried it indoors.

Nixon woke the next morning as I was hauling him fireman style through the woods. The sun was in the sky and the snows were waning.

"Where the Hell are we?" he said in a raspy voice.

"Hush now, Willie. I'll give you a sip of water when we get there."

"Where you taking me, you bastard?"

"Now, now, Willie. That ain't no way to thank a man who tended to your wounds."

Nixon held one hand then the other stump up to his face to see where I had cleaned and bandaged his amputated parts. Least, I assumed he did, since his face was hanging down toward my rear end.

"Put me down and let me die."

"All in good time, Willie. Do you know what time of year it is?"

"Huh?"

"It's closing in on spring."

"So? Ain't going gatoring with these hands now."

I paused, a wonderful sight spread out before us. The mighty frozen river. I swung around to give him a look at it.

"You see that, Willie? Ain't that a sight to behold?"

He didn't answer, so I stepped gingerly onto the ice, testing to see it would take our weight. Thank the Lord it did, and I motioned out like Jesus, carrying my burden.

When I reached the spot I'd carefully picked out, I laid him gently on the ice. Then I dropped the ropes off my shoulder.

"What…what are you doing?"

"You never stuck around the river during the winter, Willie. Not once."

"So damn cold."

"Look around you. What do you see?

Nixon craned his neck, did his best to scan the frozen waters. "Ice, just ice, and a few dead trees stickin' up."

I smiled. "They ain't trees, Willie. Look closer."

He did, and it was as if he cottoned on to what I was about all at once.

"No! They…that can't be."

"It is. You ever heard the term, brumation, Willie?"

He shook his head.

I picked him up under the shoulders and held my canteen to his lips. Then I lifted him upright and started tying him to the tree. He was too weak to fight me, as I'd planned.

"In the winter time, gators don't hibernate like some other critters. They got a unique system shuts their body down, but they still need to breathe. So, when the river starts icing up, they prop themselves up like you see right there, with their snouts sticking out of the ice. That my friend, is what they call brumation. I learned that from an old gator man."

Nixon looked around desperately at all the gator snouts propped up in the ice.

"You can't leave me here."

I ignored him and tightened the ropes. Then I took a few steps back and looked up at the bright sun.

"Zeke, I know I done wrong. I repent." Drool ran down his chin and his eyes looked fit to burst.

"I ain't no preacher, Willie, no holy man, 'cept I can walk on water." I started to walk away across the ice.

Nixon called after me, "Kill me, Zeke. Cut me with your knife. I deserve it…please, Zeke."

I turned and gave him one last sermon.

"I offer you the same quality of mercy you showed them girls and my unborn, Willie. Them gators look frozed to death, but they ain't. Soon as the snows thaw, those big critters will spring right back to life. I figure they'll be a mite hungry, and them teeth look sharper than any knife."

* * *

That's my story about what happened 'tween me and Willie Nixon. Never did figure out what was wrong in that man's head that made him do those awful things. I know what I did in return weren't nice neither, but I figure I was justified. An eye for an eye, the Good Book says. Never told no one my tale till now. In time, my heart healed some and I found myself a new woman. She bore me two children who grew up fine and strong. I went back to gatoring till I couldn't cut no more. Never heard a thing 'bout Willie Nixon again, and no part of him ever did come floating on the tide past my boat.

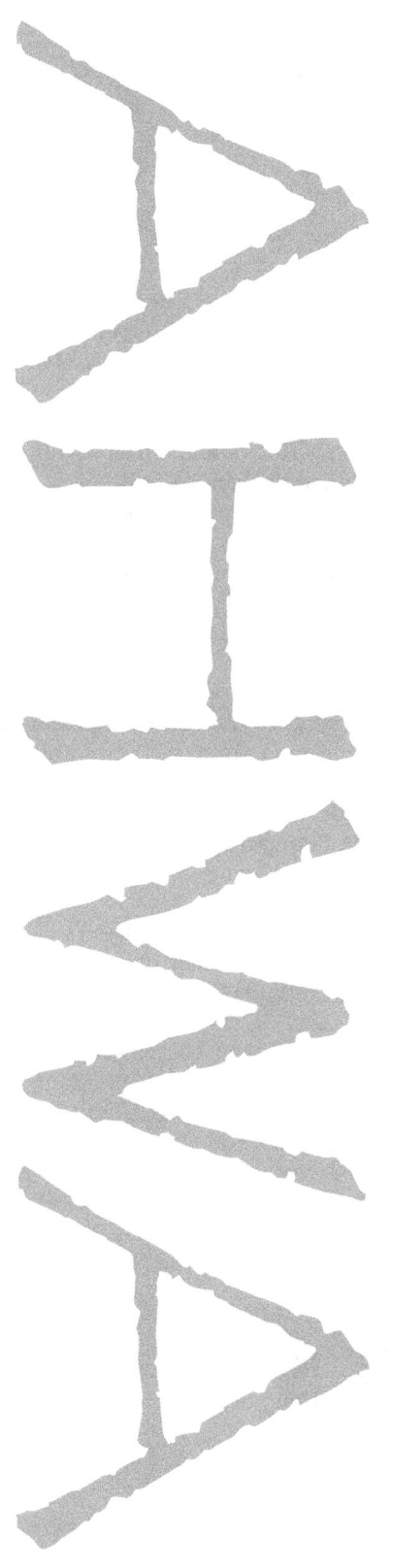

CONGRATULATIONS
TO THE WINNERS OF THE
2019 AUSTRALIAN SHADOWS AWARDS

COLLECTED WORKS
WINNER: Served Cold by Alan Baxter
Collision: Stories by J.S. Breukelaar
Figments and Fragments by Deborah Sheldon

EDITED WORKS
WINNER: Midnight Echo #14
edited by Deborah Sheldon
Beside the Seaside: Tales from the Day-Tripper
edited by Steve Dillon
Trickster's Treats #3 – the Seven Deadly Sins Edition
edited by Marie O'Regan and Lee Murray

GRAPHIC NOVEL
WINNER: DCeased written by Tom Taylor (art by
Trevor Hairsine, Stefano Gaudiano, Laura Braga,
Richard Friend, James Harren, Darick Robertson,
Trevor Scott and Neil Edwards)
The Eldritch Kid: The Bone War written by Christian
D. Read (art by Paul Mason)
Matinee written by Emmet O'Cuana (art by David
Parsons)
Geebung Polo Club written by Jason Fischer
(adapted from a Banjo Patterson poem), (art by
Shauna O'Meara)

THE ROCKY WOOD AWARD FOR NON-FICTION AND CRITICISM
WINNER: The Danse Macabre by Kyla Lee Ward
Suffer the Little Children by Kris Ashton
Horror and the paranormal, chapter 8 of Writing
Speculative Fiction by Eugen Bacon
Horror Movies That Mean Something and
Childhood Trauma Manifested by Maria Lewis

PAUL HAINES AWARD FOR LONG FICTION
WINNER: Supermassive Black Mass
by Matthew R. Davis
The Netherwhere Line by Matthew J. Morrison
Out of Darkness by Chris Mason
The Enemy of the Enemy by Rick Kennett
1862 by C.J. Halbard

POETRY
WINNER: Taxonomy of Captured Roses
by Hester J. Rook
Brine and Vanishings by Hester J. Rook
Please Do Not Feed the Animals by Anne Casey
Separation by Jay Caselberg
Ode to a Black Hole by Charles Lovecraft
Boat of a Million Years by Kyla Lee Ward

SHORT FICTION
WINNER: Steadfast Shadowsong
by Matthew R. Davis
Vivienne & Agnes by Chris Mason
The Ocean Hushed the Stones by Alan Baxter
Ava Rune by J.S. Breukelaar

NOVEL
WINNER: Shepherd by Catherine Jinks
Fusion by Kate Richards
The Flower and the Serpent by Madeleine D'Este

A SECOND CHANCE
BY MELANIE HARDING-SHAW

I crouched to pick up the single yellow and white thread from the dirt on the side of the road. I held it close to my nose to inhale its scent, half expecting it to smell of the lemons printed on the apron's fabric. But, of course, it did not. It smelled of scared child and dust burning on an overheated radiator.

I placed the thread on my tongue and swallowed it. It did nothing to fill the hole that she had left. It tasted of broken dreams and the vanilla ice cream that had dripped down her fingers before she could eat it.

The road ran across the landscape like a ribbon inexpertly sewn around the hem of a pinafore, bunching in places where the road workers could not be bothered taming the rolling dunes. They liked the idea of the road but lacked the patience to follow through. I had lacked patience when sewing the apron, but only to ensure that her little fingers could more easily drop a trail of threads for me to follow.

My footprints stretched behind me in the red clay. On the days when a squall moved in with bursts of rain, the earth's pigment leached into the water and each drop became a splash of blood on the remains of my trail. Squalling weather, squalling child. Some days it felt like I really was bleeding out. Those were the days of harsh sunlight and the sandpaper of rubbing the crystallised salt of my sweat from my face.

Until the soles of my shoes gave out. Then I bled for real.

* * *

I feel every thread I've found writhing in my belly. Does she have butterflies in her tummy as she senses me growing closer? I have their larvae. The acid of my stomach will liquefy them, and I will be a walking chrysalis, a living icon of rebirth, of a thousand rebirths. Perhaps in one, I will find her.

Only, I am no longer walking. There are no more threads to find. The trail is gone and so is my heart.

I am lying gasping for air on the road. There is a shadow in the distance. I like to think it is the car in which she flees. It gives me comfort to think she is close at the end. I would have been a good mother to the child. She could have been mine.

The writhing has changed now. My back arches against the rough gravel and my mouth stretches wide. I have drawn my last breath. As the darkness sets in, my final exhalation swirls from deep inside me, a swarm of lemon cotton butterflies bursting past my jaws to freedom.

* * *

A little girl sits on the side of the road as her mother fills the radiator with shaking hands, one eye always on the road behind them.

"Mama, look," she says. On her finger perches a single yellow pinafore butterfly.

By the time her mother turns, it has already disappeared inside her mouth.

THE MIDNIGHT SONG
BY STUART OLVER
AHWA SHORT STORY COMPETITION WINNER 2019

Justin strode along the dark-hour streets, clutching the hand of his young son tightly. He tasted the city as a banquet, laid out over glass and stone and macadam, stewing in and rich with the colour and sound of humanity. The hour was late, and the eateries were beginning to close, their last patrons spilling out to share the sidewalk with Justin and Liam.

The people seemed flirtatious and tipsy. Justin couldn't remember having had a drink, yet he struggled to recall why he and Liam were out so late, and where exactly they were heading. Up ahead was the central train station, and that seemed the right place to be, although Justin felt as if they'd been going in circles.

Midnight stragglers led the way inside. But this entrance was small, subterranean, opening to swallow them as if the city was tasting them. There were so many tunnels, and people pushed past them in their haste, disappearing around corners, until Justin and Liam arrived at a junction, all alone. In a moment's indecision, Justin heard it, faintly, coming from the right branch: a woman's voice over an even fainter guitar. And without any specific reason why, he turned and guided Liam towards the sound.

The graffiti on the walls of the tunnel was dense, a tortured mishmash of greens and oranges that throbbed against his eyeballs. The walls whispered at their passing, and their footfalls squeaked against the tiles, the echoes making it seem like they were surrounded by dozens of other people. Liam dragged on Justin's arm. He looked down;

his son whimpered, his eyes wide with fear.

"What's wrong, buddy?"

Liam shook his head, making urgent little sounds with his throat, though no actual words came out.

"Liam, don't be silly, please," said Justin. "We need to go this way to get home."

Liam stared at him, then blinked and walked forward, although his steps were leaden.

There was a sudden burst of white light, and they emerged from the tunnel onto a platform crammed with commuters. The contrast between the deserted tunnel and the bustling platform couldn't have been more startling, especially as there'd been no gradual brightening of the light ahead of them. The jostling throng tasted like iron filings at the back of Justin's throat.

There was a train already on the platform, but no-one was getting off or on. Against a column, a woman sat on a padded milk crate, brown hair draping her shoulders as she bent over a burnished acoustic guitar. Her voice found the notes, pure and effortless. Justin recognised the song. It was 'Blue Jay Way' by the Beatles. Justin had never heard it played acoustically, and, as the tune rose to its refrain, the taste in his mouth turned to buttered corn-on-the-cob. Several commuters passed by without a glance, and Justin was struck by the curious and unsettling notion that the woman was invisible to all but him and Liam.

The woman stopped playing, then looked at Justin and smiled.

Embarrassed at being caught staring, he

walked up to her, fumbling for his wallet. There was only silver in the coin pouch, so, after a moment's hesitation, he gave Liam a ten dollar note, the smallest denomination he had. His son stared at him with unblinking eyes, before shuffling forward to limply drop the money into the basket.

"Why, thank you," she said, "I'm Ofelia. And you are...?"

"Oh…I'm Justin, and this is Liam…nice to meet you." Justin extended his hand, and she took it. Her skin was cool and dry, despite the clammy air around the platform.

"You're very generous. I like that." Ofelia rose and tousled Liam's curls. The boy stared mutely at her; Justin couldn't recall him saying anything for quite a while.

Ofelia indicated the guitar. "Do you play, Justin?"

"Yes, but not to your level."

Ofelia stared intently at Liam for a moment, before shaking her head slightly, and focussing back on Justin. "Where are you headed?" she asked.

"Towards the south-west. But we're a bit lost, to be honest."

"Follow me." Ofelia packed her guitar into its case, then strode to the edge of the platform and stepped through the open side door of the train. "We have to be quick," she said over her shoulder.

Justin and his son squeezed through the door, which immediately slid closed behind them. Ofelia pushed her way towards the middle of the carriage, and Justin and Liam followed. Every seat, it seemed, was occupied; every face turning their way. Justin managed to find an empty space beside an elderly woman. Ofelia refused the offered seat, so Justin helped Liam into it. Justin grabbed a handrail, and within seconds a sudden jerk signalled that the train was underway.

The passengers in the carriage had stopped staring and were all now cocooned in their own private worlds. They tapped and swiped their fingers on their smartphones, a nervous energy to their movements. Several of the commuters were shaking. The train entered a tunnel, and light from the carriage weakly illuminated the grey walls rushing by outside.

Ofelia was standing very close to Justin. Only the guitar case wedged between her knee and his kept them from bumping against each other as the train rocked along the tracks. Ofelia smiled, although her eyes flitted about the carriage. Several times, she gazed at Liam. Only when Justin asked a question did she properly look at him.

"Which station are you getting off at?" he said, hoping the name would trigger some recognition regarding his own destination, which, for the life of him, he just couldn't bring to mind.

"There are no stations in the tunnel," said Ofelia obliquely. Before Justin could ask her to elaborate, the train shuddered to a halt. The people standing behind Justin fell against him, grinding his knee painfully against the guitar case. He let out a little gasp and looked around. The passengers' eyes were fixed on the sliding doors connecting this carriage to the one behind.

Justin looked at Ofelia, and she put a finger to her lips. Justin became aware of the faint thudding of his heart. Liam, meanwhile, slumped in his seat. Then, there was a barely perceptible forward motion, before the train stuttered along the tracks, gaining momentum. People exchanged glances, or a few quiet words, before settling back with their screens.

"What was that all about?" Justin asked quietly.

"Sometimes the train stops," said Ofelia,

"And then we must be quiet."

"Oh, is this a designated quiet carriage?" Justin said, "I'm sorry, I didn't know."

A muffled sob came from nearby. In the seat opposite, a young couple sat stiffly holding hands. Silent tears rolled down the girl's face. Justin looked around, at the downcast eyes and slumped shoulders of the passengers. On the last row of seats, near the rear doors, a lone elderly man dabbed at his eyes with a handkerchief.

Justin faced Ofelia with a frown, but she was kneeling to take her guitar out of its case. She fitted the strap over her shoulders and played, quietly at first, and then with bright, clear tones. Her fingers glided over the strings, combining chords and notes into a beguiling melody. Justin tasted rather than heard the music. It was as if his mouth was awash with a full-bodied red wine, and though others might speak of hints of dark chocolate, anise, eucalyptus or blackberry, Justin couldn't identify specific flavours, only that they worked together to bring the most delicious sensation to his palate.

He didn't know how long Ofelia continued to play, but suddenly he was clutching at the handrail of the adjacent seat, as if startled out of a dream. Liam and the elderly woman were asleep, his son's head resting against the woman's shoulder. He glanced up and down the carriage; the other passengers were asleep or nodding off. Those who'd been standing in the aisle slumped over one another on the floor. Only the old man regarded them with rheumy eyes.

Ofelia gave Justin a soft, sad smile. "The music helps, a little…" And she went on playing.

Justin was finding it hard to stay awake. But he was jerked back to consciousness when the train shuddered to a stop a second time.

Ofelia sighed deeply and stopped playing.

"What's going on?" asked Justin, ignoring her warning glance to stay quiet. "Why is everyone asleep?" A cold chill gripped his body.

"Try to understand," said Ofelia, "Sometimes, it's better to be asleep than to hear the silence."

And with that, a most peculiar taste arose in his mouth. It was not unlike sucking candy, the type that is incredibly sour until the sweet centre is reached; the type that Justin struggled to eat and yet found irresistible at the same time. The flavour became almost unbearable as its astringency built, always with a hint of the sweetness that might come. He gagged.

"What's wrong?" Ofelia asked.

"A taste…a taste in my mouth…bitter…sour…but I can't hear anything."

Ofelia frowned, so he continued, spitting out words as if he could also rid himself of the taste.

"I have a condition—a rare form of synaesthesia. Different sounds cause me to sense distinct tastes in my mouth. It's unpredictable…but it mainly happens with sustained sounds…like music, for example."

"It's singing! All this time, and I didn't guess!" said Ofelia, her eyes ablaze, "Your brain isn't processing it as a sound that you can hear, but as something you can taste."

"What is singing?"

Ofelia gave a little cry. "Oh, no, not him."

Behind Justin, the old man had risen from his seat, and was moving stiffly towards the sliding doors leading to the aft carriage.

"We have to stop him!" said Ofelia. She put down her guitar and led Justin, gently but firmly, towards the back of the carriage.

Too overwhelmed by the taste to resist, Justin stumbled over the prone passengers. The old man placed his hands and face against the glass panels of the doors, seemingly in a trance. The underlying hint of sweetness strengthened in Justin's mouth.

Drawing him closer…

Somewhere in there, beyond the doors, was the core of sweetness that would take away the agony.

The old man pressed a button, and the doors slid open. He moved through the narrow vestibule and opened the doors to the next carriage. The light stopped at this portal, and the space beyond was inky black. Without hesitation, the old man stepped through and disappeared. Justin moved to follow him.

"Maybe you shouldn't…" said Ofelia.

But fear had yielded to an irresistible compulsion to find out what was beyond that black veil. The acrid taste was fast being replaced by an exquisite sweetness, like the purest, lightest honey. He felt forwards in the darkness, blinded to all but the sensation on his palate, which led him on as if he were a snake tasting prey. His vision adjusted, until he could actually see the old man, although the image was fuzzy, like watercolour paint on damp paper. It was emanating light from an unknown source. The old man was moving further down the carriage, which in the darkness seemed unbounded by any physical frame.

Justin followed, the last vestiges of the sour taste disappearing. He couldn't feel any seats or handholds, but the air in the carriage brushed against him as he walked, as if parting to let him enter. He began to make out other people, blurs of muted colour at first, then brightening like they were illuminated from within.

But something was terribly wrong. They were suspended in the dark, limp and lifeless, heads and arms and legs at unnatural angles, skin blotchy, and clothing ragged.

Justin reached out to touch the shoulder of the old man. "Come back. Don't go on."

The man slowly turned and shook his head. "Please," he said, "I'm so very tired."

Ghastly figures surrounded them, moving imperceptibly, drifting on gentle air currents…*or swaying to a melody*. Justin's mouth was coated in luscious characters of butterscotch and caramel, but beneath it all there was a cloying consistency. And he noticed more and more the decay in the figures that approached. Stripped flesh and atrophied muscles. Features melting off faces. The air was hot and damp, and in one terrifying moment Justin saw himself like the others, the moisture beading on his skin, dissolving him.

He sensed the crescendo of the song. His nerves were made of spun sugar, and yet the sweetness couldn't mask the unmistakable funk of putrefying flesh.

Turning away from the bodies, he searched blindly for the entrance. The old man was forgotten, vanished. Justin caught a hint of bitterness on his tongue, and stumbled forwards. He called out to Ofelia but got no reply. The candied flavour developed a sour thread. He thumped against something hard, found a button, and burst from the darkness into the lit vestibule.

Ofelia was no longer standing in the doorway.

Justin re-entered the original carriage, the taste gone from his mouth.

At the far end of the carriage, Ofelia cradled a sleeping Liam in her arms. She was sobbing, and looked up, terrified, as Justin made his way towards her.

"It's ok," he said, but she shrank back, almost stumbling over a young man who was slumped against one of the seats.

"Get away!" she cried.

"But you've got my son, Ofelia."

"Your…your son? No! He's my son!"

"What are you talking about?" Justin advanced another step

Ofelia backed up against the doors to the forward carriage. Hidden behind standing passengers, Justin hadn't noted those doors prior to now; all the attention had been on the doors at the other end of the carriage. Where did this portal lead? To another carriage? To other passengers?

"You stole my son, and now you're trying to take him away from me again!" Fury rose in Ofelia's voice. She clutched Liam even tighter, and he woke up.

"Ofelia, you know Liam's not your son. You must remember that he came on board with me." Justin raised his arms, palms outward, but Ofelia spun and hit the button for the sliding doors. Justin sprang forward but stumbled over a sleeping passenger. As he rose, Ofelia and Liam disappeared into the darkness of the forward carriage.

The sliding doors closed behind them.

In an instant, Justin was at the doors. But the moment he pushed the button to open them, the sour taste sprang up in his mouth again.

He stumbled across the small vestibule, through the second set of sliding doors. "Ofelia! Liam!"

His words sounded dull, absorbed by something. Desperately, he willed his eyes to accustom to the dark. Another few steps, and the astringency increased.

Ofelia had believed that his conjoined senses were picking up some sort of tune. Which meant something…*but, by God, what*…was singing. The song had tasted sweeter the closer he'd come to the singer in the previous carriage.

An idea came to him in a flash. What if the sweet and sour tastes were the result of

his brain registering more than one sound? Maybe there were two Songs. Songs that competed with one another to ensnare the unwary. Did Ofelia's guitar tunes dull the effect of the Songs? Or protect her in some way? By lulling the passengers to sleep, did she prevent their escape? Or ensure her guitar couldn't be taken from her?

"Liam!"

Justin thought he heard a faint answer up ahead. He inched forward, trying to part the black miasma that surrounded him. But with each step, the taste increased in intensity. He could be swilling battery acid.

The song was at a crescendo. Justin couldn't go on. He bent over, retching. Hot tears ran down his cheeks.

Light flooded the carriage. Startled, Justin looked up. The platform of an underground station passed by the window. Identical to the one where he and Liam had stepped onto the train. Commuters milled about, but the train didn't stop. Within a few seconds the train entered an unlit tunnel, and darkness shrouded the carriage.

"No!" cried Justin, straightening up. He felt his way to the side sliding doors to look back at the receding station, but there wasn't the faintest glow of light.

The train flashed by another station.

Justin blinked.

Bright platform. Commuters.

Then the tunnel was upon them again, quicker than before.

Justin beat his fists against the glass. "Stop the train!"

Once again, the brief blackness gave way to sudden light: a station, a platform, people just metres away, but unreachable. The train was speeding up, each new iteration of dark tunnel and luminous platform whizzing by faster than the one before. But Justin had seen enough in the third pass of the station to know that it was merely the same scene repeated over and over again.

The light!

Justin had been so absorbed with looking out the window that he hadn't thought to examine the interior of the carriage. But by now each brief burst of ambient light barely lasted a second. Justin peered down the empty row of seats; Ofelia could be holding his son down behind one of them. "Liam! Ofelia!"

Movement, momentarily revealed by the glow of light from outside: Ofelia and Liam, ducking from one row of seats into the next. Justin ran for them as the rapid transition between light and dark became a strobing effect. Ofelia and Liam seemed to move in slow motion as they changed direction and walked towards him. Despite the agonisingly bitter taste in his mouth, Justin's heart spiked in elation at the thought that Ofelia might be bringing his son back to him.

Then Liam screamed, and Justin's sanity unravelled.

From the superposition of light and dark, the singer of the Song emerged. Like nothing that could be imagined, and yet every nightmare that could be dreamt up, it inhabited the very fabric of the carriage, yet was not bound by it. It was both unfathomable darkness and blazing with rapacity and malevolence. It was an agony of timelessness, a dealer of instantaneous slaughter. And it advanced with mocking sluggishness as Ofelia and Liam ran jerky in the strobing light.

The look in Liam's eyes galvanized him. Coughing and spitting, Justin ran to his son and grabbed his arm. He pulled him back towards the sliding doors.

Ofelia dragged on Liam's other arm.

One of them found the button, and they stumbled across the vestibule into the lighted carriage. The passengers had begun to wake, and many were on their feet. They crowded the side entrance door. It was wide open. Though the darkness was surely rushing by outside, every one of them jumped out.

Without fail, they were thrown back.

Ofelia weaved through the bodies, clutching Liam to her chest, and Justin barely hung on to one arm. At the yawning opening, Ofelia turned to face Justin. He grabbed Liam's shoulders, and his little boy opened his eyes and mouth wide and screamed, lashing Justin's ears and pouring fire on his tongue. Liam scrabbled to rip Justin's hands away; he kicked out with his legs, pushing into Ofelia.

Woman and child teetered on the edge of the door.

Justin felt his grip weakening. He wanted to say *Don't let go*, but as the agonised words tumbled from his mouth, they changed. "Don't go…"

Then Liam's teeth found his knuckles, Justin's fingers lost their hold, and Ofelia and the boy fell backwards into the darkness. The sliding doors snapped together as tight as a trap.

Now on their feet, everyone else turned to Justin, mouths gaping blackness, silent screams pouring like a torrent at him. Ofelia's guitar case was where she'd left it. He picked it up and swung it like a shield. He forced his way back into the black acid embrace of the forward carriage, seeking sweet oblivion. But he was barely inside when the carriage fractured like a million-faceted kaleidoscope. Each infinitesimal piece of light and dark showered him with cruel, cascading laughter.

Empty space before him, the dirt bit at his skin as the train shrieked into the tunnel.

Still clutching the guitar case, and guided by cold steel rail alone, Justin eventually found his way into an underground station. But not before his sanity had unravelled like string pulled back along the tunnel.

* * *

The seat was comfortable; the burnished guitar felt familiar in his hands. Justin looked briefly at the rail commuters scurrying about the platform before beginning to play. He was halfway through 'Long Promised Road' by the Beach Boys when he spotted a woman and young boy watching him. He nodded and smiled at them.

Embarrassed at being caught staring, the woman fumbled for her purse. After she'd rummaged a few moments, she gave a ten dollar note to the boy. He stared at Justin with unblinking eyes, before shuffling forward to limply drop the money into the basket.

"Why, thank you," he said, "I'm Justin. And you are…?"

"Oh…I'm Ofelia, and this is Liam…nice to meet you." She extended her hand, and he took it. But his eyes were drawn to Liam, whose face stirred his memory like colour percolating on a Polaroid.

"You're very generous. I like that," said Justin. He indicated the guitar. "Do you play, Ofelia?"

"Yes, but not to your level."

Justin smiled. "Where are you headed?" he asked.

"Towards the south-west. But it feels like we've been going round in circles, to be honest."

"Follow me." Justin packed his guitar into its case, and then strode to the edge of the platform and stepped onto the train.

"We have to be quick," he said over his shoulder.

Ofelia and Liam squeezed through the door.

Immediately, it slid closed behind them.

LITTLE SPOON
BY ALISSA SMITH
AHWA FLASH FICTION COMPETITION WINNER 2019

I love being the 'little spoon'. Nestled against Christopher's body with his arm hooked over my waist. His firm pecs touch my bare back and his rock-hard thighs press against my buttocks. His fingers form a perfect cup around my left breast.

I whisper sweet words to Christopher. He is quiet in his slumber, but I'm not discouraged. He's a wonderful companion. I'm content in his arms.

Our first encounter has been sensational. Shedding my clothes, layer by layer, in a slow and titillating performance. The excitement of seeing Christopher's nakedness; the contours of his physique illuminated by the pale light.

We've been lying here for almost an hour. The room is cold and there's only a thin sheet over our bodies. I can't fall asleep. *Shouldn't* fall asleep. I must get up now.

With as little disturbance as possible, I slip smoothly from under Christopher's arm. It's like a dead weight. His body shifts slightly as I stand, but his eyes remain closed. In the dim light, his face looks peaceful.

Shivering from the cold, I pick up my pile of work clothes and get dressed quickly. Then I wander the rows of small drawers, searching for my next undertaking. Here: this is the one.

I open the small stainless steel door. The toe-tag says his name was Brad.

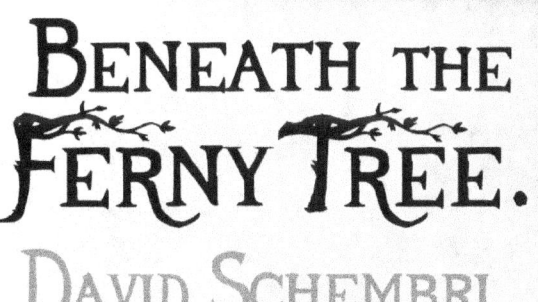

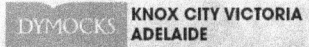

A Vindication of Monsters:
Essays on Mary Shelley and Mary Wollstonecraft.

Deadline: December 1st, 2020
Wordcount: Up to 5,000 words. Query for longer.
Payment: $50
Email submissions to: claire.fitzpatrick1991@gmail.com

MY CLAIRE
BY DAVID SCHEMBRI

Anyone else would think it was a miracle. To have a loved one return to you. Sure, I admit I was happy to see her, hoping her death had been some horrible mistake. Perhaps she didn't get drunk that night with her friends and go swimming in that river. Maybe Claire didn't drown. The current could've taken her far down stream, you know, beyond the span of the search party. It's not unheard of that people can grab a floating log and keep their head above water, is it? I wasn't a fool to be so optimistic. That's what sprang to mind when she rapped on my door in the late hours, saying, "Poppy, I'm back!"

However, my Claire is not a miracle.

She's just another of the Lost who won't rest.

* * *

"Hold still!" I said through gritted teeth.

"It hurts."

"That's just confusing. How the bloody hell can anything hurt you?"

With a final tug, the axe came free from its wedge of brain and bone. I set the bloodied tool down and held back the urge to retch; blobs of brain matter clung to the blade and glistened eerily in the firelight. The smell was worse, believe it or not. Imagine rotting fish mixed with mouldy cheese, and you would see what I mean.

Bile rose in my throat as she fingered the split in her head. "Would you stop doing that? You're making me sick!"

"Can you stitch it up for me?" she asked.

Her eyes, although cataract-grey, still somehow held that glimmer of her former self. She'd been a cheeky teenager and had always managed to get me to do things with that look of hers. I fool you not; there was a time she had me out with my rifle one cold night to check there were no intruders trying to pry open her window. She was good to be nervous. It made her careful; after all, she'd inherited her late mother's good looks—pity her nerves never told her that booze and swimming didn't go together.

"Stitches? What good will *that* do you? It won't heal. You should've listened to me and stayed in the barn!"

"Is that it for me then, Poppy? I'm just to stay out there? Why can't I stay in the house with you?"

The funny thing was, even though she was dead, she was still as sensitive a soul as ever. I didn't have the heart to tell her that she reeked. When she'd first arrived, the decomposition had yet to reveal the yellowing pus that dripped from her nose. Her greening, peeling skin, the bloating that had formed in her neck, and of course, the decay shrinking her cheeks.

"It's safer for you out there, you know, in case people come knocking." I sighed and washed my hands at the sink, watching the blood dilute across the day-old dishes; she always used to do them for me.

"Are you mad at me, Poppy?" she asked, sitting up from the kitchen table.

"Good guess. It's not every day one's granddaughter is waiting for you when you return from ploughing the fields, with an axe wedged in her skull. You're lucky the bastard didn't take your head off!" I said as I spun and locked eyes with her. "Did anyone see you? Do I have to ready my rifle?"

"No, it was just him. He was alone, you see.

Working on that nice car of his."

"You stupid girl," I hissed.

"I'm sorry, Poppy. I couldn't help it. I could smell him a mile away!"

"That's the minister's son out there! Sprawled in the mud with a gaping hole in his neck! You know the law: '*If the dead return, bring them now to burn*'." I raked fingers through my thinning, grey hair and nodded. "If the townsfolk find out I kept you; they'll burn us both. Together, in Main Street, as an example. It's a tradition they still hold to now. Didn't you learn anything in school?"

"I'm sorry, Poppy…"

I sighed. "Why did you have to do it? Why run the risk of exposing us?"

She shrugged, scratching the back of her decaying neck. "I was hungry, Poppy."

"I told you to feast on my sheep and cattle."

"It's not the same. They're like bad milk to me, not like—" She turned a longing gaze to the back door, obviously yearning for the Minister's son's carcass, waiting for her in the mud. "—like him."

"I'm going to throw up…" I faced away from her, took deep, calming breaths before turning back. "Where's the granddaughter I use to love? That's why I couldn't let the mob find you."

"She died in the river. You know that. But Poppy, I'm still here. It's still me. I'm just different, is all. I promise I'll try and be good."

"But you won't change."

"I wish I could, but I can't. Only now, I understand why all others like me couldn't change. They have no real choice; the hunger just won't go away."

"Well, you better get to it then," I said, turning away from her and resting both hands on the sink.

"Does that mean I can keep him?"

"Evidence is in my backyard, so yes, you get to keep him. But, on one condition."

"Anything, Poppy."

"You eat everything. Right down to the bones. There must not be *anything* left to find. Got it?"

"Yes, Poppy," she said, making for the back door.

"Claire?"

She snapped a look at me; the hunger in her grey eyes reflected the emerging monster—the thing that would remain, leaving no trace of the granddaughter I loved.

"The town will be searching for that lad. You're never to leave that barn again, okay?"

"What about my next meal?" she said in a voice deeper than normal. A drop of thick drool fell from the corner of her mouth. A mouth that commonly enjoyed a coat of pink lipstick, only then to resort to flaky skin and darkening ulcers.

My mouth went dry. "D-don't worry about that. Go and have your dinner."

I watched her drag the minister's son to the barn, the grunt of her exertion carried through to the kitchen window like a sickly gasp of a starving wolf.

She feasted for hours.

Every crunch of bone was like a nail in my heart. With each tear of flesh, images flooded of snapping teeth digging into raw meat; cracks forming in the once-perfect picture I had of her.

There was enough time for me to chain the barn doors.

To pour the fuel.

TOLERANCE TO IRON
BY JASON FRANKS

When Colin came into the room, Alison was sitting on the bed with her knees tucked up to her chest, facing the open window. He stifled a yawn and shrugged his dressing gown higher up onto his shoulders. "Are you all right, honey?"

"Daddy, there's a scary man outside." She didn't turn when she spoke to him.

Colin went to the window and made a show of peering through the glass. The yard was empty. Getting a bit unkempt, if he was honest. "I don't see any scary man, honey."

He closed the window and drew the curtain.

"I don't know if he's really a man," said Alison. "He's only little."

Colin pulled down the bedspread for her. "It's just the night, Ali. Do you remember what night is for?"

"Night is where the spaceships travel."

"That's right. At night, the sky is huge and bright with stars."

"And the moon, Daddy?" It was a litany he'd taught her to assuage the night terrors, and it had been successful for nearly a year, now. Colin hoped they weren't coming back.

"The moon is bright with sunlight." Colin offered Alison the plush rocket ship toy, and she gave it a cuddle. "Come on, it's sleeping time."

Alison snuggled down under the covers. "He's there in the daytime, too," she said. "Sometimes."

"Who? The scary man?"

"Sometimes, he's not scary."

"There's no little man outside," said Colin. "And if there was, he's the one who should be scared."

"Why should he be scared?"

"Because we know he's not real." Colin frowned and leaned close. "Also, because little men are scared of rocket ships." He made engine noises and flew the rocket in a loop-de-loop above her bed.

Alison giggled. He patted her shoulder and she turned over to face away from him.

Colin closed Alison's door behind him and stood for a moment in the hall. He could hear Netty snoring from their bedroom. Colin sighed. Maybe he'd try sleeping on the couch.

It was much cooler downstairs. Colin crossed the lounge, stepping carefully over the play mat and the plastic zoo spread across it. He went to the window and parted the blinds. As he thought—the window was open a few inches. He had cranked it halfway shut when he saw movement.

Colin peered through the blinds. Clouds hid the sickle moon, but something about the uncertain light drew his eye to the old beech tree by the swing set. Sitting in its pale and reaching limbs was a little man.

At distance, it was hard to tell how tall the little man was, but Colin didn't think it could be more than four feet high. The figure had a luminous face and a mouth full of gleaming teeth. A pair of pointed ears fixed at different angles protruded from the tangle of its hair. It was dressed in dark garments that had a formal, old-fashioned look.

Colin blinked a couple of times, but the little man was still there. He exhaled hard, shook his head, and let the fear crystallise into anger. That little bastard. Sitting in his garden, scaring his baby girl.

Colin kept the twelve-gauge on the top

shelf in the closet in the hall, behind a pile of china crockery his mother had left him. The ammunition was in the kitchen cupboard, also on the top shelf. He had to use Netty's folding step to reach the box of shells.

Colin had both barrels loaded when he came out the back door. The spring air was cold, and he was feeling a little foolish now.

It was brighter outside than he had expected. The moon must have come out, although he couldn't locate it when he squinted up into the sky. Colin waded towards the beech tree through the knee-high grass. Runners caught at his slippers, but he forged on. He wondered how the lawn had grown so quickly—he had mowed it that weekend past.

There was no sign of the little man.

Colin stopped, the gun in both hands, and stared at the tree. His shins itched from grass scratches. He took a deep breath, let it out. The breeze was up, and he could smell the hyacinths from over his neighbour's fence.

The creak of the side gate made him jump. Colin turned, bringing up the gun, just in time to see the gate snick shut. He stumbled towards it, cursing. Colin had to tuck the shotgun under one arm while he turned the handle and raised the latch. He pushed the gate open hard and stepped through.

He looked up and down the street. It was lined with double-storey houses much like his own, set back from the road and separated by fences, hedges, tall trees. Light from the streetlamps shone off family sedans and SUVs.

There was no one about. The houses were dark, including his own. He was certain he'd left the porch light on, but he couldn't see it when he looked behind him. He wasn't even sure which one was his house, now. Was this panic?

A crouching figure, dressed all in black, waited at the end of the block. The little man turned, looked over its shoulder at Colin, and scampered towards the strip mall up the road. Colin lumbered after him, his dressing gown flapping, holding the shotgun awkwardly in both hands.

The night took on a strange quality. Colin thought the moon had finally shown itself, but he still couldn't find it in the sky. He'd only looked up for a moment, but it was long enough for the little man to disappear.

Colin pressed on. If he didn't find the little man, what then? Suddenly, he felt self-conscious, waving a shotgun in the street in his gown and slippers. What would the neighbours say? The police? Netty?

But Netty wasn't there. Nor were the neighbours, nor the police. It was just him and his quarry and the moon above.

Now the cars seemed older in the strange light, rusting and derelict. Tree limbs waved overhead, and the streetlamps swivelled after him as he rushed down the street. The crown of the road rose until its curvature was visible.

Night is where the spaceships travel. That was what he'd told Alison. The night sky was not a place of darkness, it was a place full of stars and planets and rockets and wonders. And the moon. Night was where the moon lived, although you could sometimes see it in the daylight. Just like the little man.

The moon was bright with sunlight-on one side.

The little man resolved as if through an adjustment of a lens in a camera. It glanced back at Colin, then ducked into an alley behind a boarded-up florist, slinging itself into the turn and sliding out again like an ice-skater braking.

Colin rushed after it, his slippers skidding

in the slick of a puddle. When had it rained? He turned into the alley, the shotgun stock in the crook of his arm.

It was a dead-end; reeking and littered with garbage. Broken glass and empty McDonald's wrappers. The walls were stained, and filthy water dripped from a low-hanging drainpipe.

The little man was cowering in the narrow gap between the wall and a plastic dumpster. Up close it looked even stranger than it had from afar: its head was too big, its eyes too widely set. The garment Colin had taken for a frock coat was tattered and fraying, patched with strips of garbage bin liners.

"Please don't hurt me."

Colin glared down the length of the shotgun. "What are you?"

The little man's eyes were very big and wet. "We were called the Sìth, in the old country, because they thought we lived under the hills. And some of us did…but mostly we lived in the forests."

"Sìth?" Colin tried and failed to pronounce the word.

"They called us children, too," said the little man. "Though few among us were young, even in the days when we were many."

"Well, you're no child, and this is no forest. Or, you know. Old country."

"True," said the little man. "We came to this land on those big wooden boats, same as your people, all those many years ago."

"Come out here, where I can see you."

The little man edged from its hiding place, keeping its soft little hands up.

"What do you want? What were you doing in my yard?"

"Dying, mostly." A tear rolled down the little man's cheek. The Sìth was more pathetic than frightening, and even smaller than Colin had first thought. Three-and-a-half feet, tops.

"I'm sorry to hear it," said Colin. He was surprised to find that he was. He lowered the shotgun. "But you should be in the forests, if that's where you belong. Not in my yard."

"We've been driven out," said the little man. "The forests have grown thin. Your machines are everywhere, and the iron is poison to us. You destroy our homes, but you will give us no shelter."

A flush of shame warmed Colin's cheeks, although he knew he was in the right. The little man was trespassing, goddamn it. "There are…soup kitchens, hostels… I'm sure you could…"

"No," said the little man. "In the old times, your kind would hang iron on the door to keep us out. Now your homes have iron in the walls, in the ceilings, the floors."

Colin set his jaw. "That doesn't explain what you were doing in my yard."

The little man lowered its hands and held them out, trembling. "Your daughter is… sensitive. She can see us. That drew me to her."

"I can see you, too."

The little man shook its head. "Only because your Alison told you I was there. You know and love her well enough to see through her eyes, if conditions are right." The little man looked up at the sky.

Colin knew better than to take his eyes off him again. "How do you know her name?" He raised one shoulder to adjust the position of the shotgun. "How come you're here in the city, despite all the…iron, and whatever?"

The little man shrugged. "Over the years, I have built up a tolerance."

"You've…what?"

The little man smiled. "I drink small doses of it."

Colin brought up the shotgun again. "Blood." His fingers caught the triggers and the shotgun boomed.

It'd had been five years since the single occasion on which Colin had taken the weapon to the firing range, and he'd forgotten how to manage the recoil. The barrel jerked up and the shock slammed him into a brick wall. His head snapped back, and he felt it connect with the drainpipe. He wasn't sure if the ringing in his ears was from the blast or the bump.

Panting, Colin pointed the gun towards the broken corpse of the little man. It lay slumped against the dumpster. Smoke curled from its chest amidst the tattered white skin and black plastic. There was no blood.

"Oh shit, oh shit, oh shit." The gun shook in his hands.

The little man sat up. "I do not shit, and I do not bleed." Its hair was even more dishevelled than before, and its luminous face was dimpled and deformed by the buckshot. Cratered and pitted, like the surface of the moon. But the little man did not appear to be particularly upset. It shook the pellets from its hair and smiled at Colin with far too many teeth.

"You're right, of course," said the little man. "There is iron in blood, as well as magic. I would have taken some from your Alison." It shrugged, apologetic. "Just a little bit, mind you. Not enough that anyone would have noticed in the autopsy."

Colin pulled the triggers again, but he'd fired both shells already. He didn't know if it was blood dripping down his neck, or water from the drainpipe.

The little man shook its head. "You were right about all of that, but this…" It pushed the gun away with one pale hand and moved in. "*This* was a mistake."

Colin tried to step back but hit his head on the drainpipe again. His vision tilted and shifted and then he was sitting with his back against the wall of the alley.

The little man seemed taller from this new perspective. The skin of its face had smoothed again. Only the shredded clothing gave any sign that it had been shot.

"I am allergic to iron, like all of the fey folk," said the little man, "but I have never, in all my many, many years, been allergic to *lead*."

Colin tried to speak, but his lips flapped together without making any sound.

"And now," said the little man, "I'm going to drink you, and then I'm going to go back to your house."

"But…you can't go in…"

The little man ran a curved talon across its teeth. It sounded like a xylophone run. "You're right." It reached out with its talon, touched it to the back of Colin's head. A tiny spot of blood showed black upon its tip. The little man licked it clean with a tongue that was also black.

"You're right again." It had definitely grown taller. "Tolerance or no, I can't go into your house, and I can hardly persuade your family to venture out, if they can barely see me…"

The little man leaned close. Its black eyes stared at Colin from a pale, but otherwise perfect facsimile of his own face. "But I am sure they'll come outside for *you*."

KEEP WALKING
BY REBECCA FRASER

You know these streets; you know this town. You've walked these
roads before,
With bootheels worn from the souls you've torn, and ground into the
floor
Of ale-soaked inns, and high school halls. Of churches, farms, and
stores—
An ageless man with a ceaseless plan to square long-forgotten scores.
Keep walking. Oh, keep walking, for our town has hollow bones,
We hang our hats on Virtue's mat, while hoarding up our stones
To hurl at those we've buried in ground forged from our lies,
With doublespeak, pretence, deceit, our longstanding disguise.
So, keep walking. Oh, keep walking, for your scales won't bear our
weight
This town's heartbeat won't survive the heat if you rattle at our gate.
Keep walking, just keep walking. There's a village yonder way,
They've a raft of folk with souls long broke—reckon they'd have deeds
to pay.
Keep walking. Show us mercy, and we'll slam the chamber door
On our wicked ways—all our yesterdays—so you won't come round
no more.
But we all know you'll keep walking, the world ageing with your gait
And when we forget, you'll make us bleed regret…when you swing
your scythe of fate.

THE DEAD MAY DANCE
BY NIKKY LEE

The first time they hang her, she laughs at them. Right up until the noose chokes the last cackle from her throat. Until her rotted feet twitch death's final dance and stillness descends.

"Do not grieve for her," Father Gavriil says to us, as we stamp and shiver in the winter chill. His face, smooth and flawless as a babe's, gleams in the dusk. "She was an abomination. She does not deserve your pity."

He is careful not to say her name. We all are. Lest she rise again.

"She killed Lady Milena, I can't believe it," Sasha, the innkeeper, whispers. "Lord Voronin must be devastated."

"Believe it," Matev mutters. "I had to help cart away Milena's corpse. There was…" He shivers in his guardsman uniform. "…not much left to bury."

"Hush, all of you," Mistress Devka hisses, her gaudy beads clacking at her neck as she rounds on us. She glances at the priests. "Not *here*." Her painted eyes turn on me, and I pull my cloak tighter as she searches my face. We've shared no more than a dozen words in all my visits to Sasha's inn, but her forehead creases, concerned nonetheless. "Olya, are you alright?"

I lie. "I'm fine. It's just—" I look up at the corpse, taking in the grave dirt still under her fingernails. "It's my first time seeing…"

It is not my first time seeing a corpse.

Devka pats my elbow. "I know you were close. But she's in a better place now." She turns back to Lapachka's village gallows and the monastery beyond it, muscles working behind her made up face. "Though I still can't believe it."

"May the Twelve rest her soul," Father Gavriil says at the head of the procession, and the crowd bows their heads with him.

"May the Twelve rest her soul," they chime. I want to laugh. *The Gods aren't listening. Not now.*

* * *

They learn the second time. They burn her at the stake. And as the priests' spellfire roars across her flesh, she screams. Not in pain, but with the anger of a soul thwarted.

The wind off Yaromir Peak catches the sound, mixing it into flurries of snow and ash, and scattering it through Lapachka's cobblestone streets. The crowd watches in chilled silence but for the breath rattling in their chests. Even Father Gavriil is quiet. His face is pale, the neck of his white and gold robe stained dark with sweat. His gaze never leaves the flames as they roar high above the rooftops.

"First Lady Milena, and now she's taken Lord Voronin, too," Sasha whispers. Her voice trembles, fear and outrage rolling into one. "*Why?*"

Matev stands beside her, listless, like an empty coat draped over a hook. His face is grey, uniform shabby and unwashed.

"You saw the corpse?" Devka asks him.

He nods, then shudders. "Work of a monster," he says. "Twelve, pray this is the end of it."

Devka looks him up and down. "I didn't take you for a convert, Matev."

He shrugs one shoulder, a sluggish half-jerk, as if too tired to do anything more. "Man's got to have hope, especially these days, what with folk going missing all over the place n' all. You know six others vanished last month before she—" He glances at the pyre, and his voice drops, "—came back. All stabbed through the heart, like she was. Captain's at his wits end—and working us half to death." He scowls. "So sue me for finding some comfort in the Twelve."

"Well," I say, staring at the flames. "At least we're one monster less." Though I know it's not true.

"I heard they found Lord Voronin in the woods, near Nemir Brook," Sasha says, gaze fixed on the pyre and the corpse writhing within it. "That's where they found *her*. The first time I mean, when she was proper dead." She shuffles closer. "Strange things are afoot up there. *Unnatural* things."

"Sasha," Devka's voice rises in warning. "Save it for your tavern."

The fire strips the corpse's flesh away, leaving nothing but bones and a thick, pungent stench of charred meat. A tug at my sleeve makes me turn. Sasha. "Doesn't Nemir Brook run through your mill?"

I nod.

She bites her lip and her brow furrows, worried. "Be careful out there."

Too late for that.

At Devka's glare, she pulls away, saving me from having to answer.

"Gods of the Twelve, rest her soul," Father Gavriil prays before us, clasping the prayer beads tight in his hands.

We bow our heads with his.

As soon as the pyre dies to glowing coals, Gavriil leaves, hauling up his ash-stained robe so he can lengthen his stride. He pushes through the crowd before they can part.

I clench my fist under my cloak, feeling the scar there. I do not move. I want him to see me. I want him to *know*.

That's right, you bastard, I'm still here.

Our eyes meet and he stops; freezing like a man who has come face to face with the Dark Reaper herself.

In a way, he has.

"Gods have mercy," the words rush out, no more than a murmur. Sweat pours down his silky skin. This close, he seems too youthful for his fifty years.

I smile and step aside. "May the Gods have mercy," I echo. *But I will not.*

He hitches up his robe and runs.

* * *

I call her name again that night.

"This is your last chance," I tell my friend as I raise her blackened bones from the graveyard.

There is only one more, she tells me.

"Then we make sure we finish it," I say and hold up my fingers. "I cannot raise your soul again." I've not known my power long, but of this I'm sure. With every summoning, her soul feels less tethered. I do not think I can bring her back a fourth time. "He's well protected." I nod to the monastery atop the distant rise. Its spires split the rising moon in two. If I listen carefully, the tramp of guard boots come on the breeze.

She cocks her skull at me, teeth trapped in a perpetual grin. *Mere men won't stop me.*

"*Magically* protected," I tell her. "He has the Gods' blessing."

Her bones shrug. *And I have yours.*

"It is not the same thing."

It is close enough. There's a tinkle of bones shifting, and the skeleton holds out a hand. *You have my thanks, Olya.*

"I am not her. Not anymore." Under my cloak, I rub the puckered flesh over my heart. My fingers search for the slow, rhythmic beat that shouldn't be there. Not since the night, nearly two moons ago, when the bag fell over my head and they dragged me, kicking and screaming, through the brush. Not since they dumped me on the earth, bound and gagged, like a huntsman's trophy.

Not since I heard Lady Melina hiss from the shadows beyond my hessian blindfold: "You brought *her*? You were supposed to take someone young. Someone supple."

Lord Voronin's voice had boomed in response, "She still has plenty of life left." After listening to his drunken rambling in Sasha's tavern on and off for ten years, I'd have recognised it anywhere. "They're not picky."

I was just a widower then. Husband dead five years to the plague. Just one woman scrounging a living from her mill, alone and with no one to miss her.

Except for one dear friend who would not stop asking questions.

Lying in the dirt, listening to Voronin and Melina squabble, I'd felt the hand fall on my shoulder and squeeze, as if it wanted to be around my throat. "She will do fine."

That was the last time my heart skipped. Hope and horror had cracked it against my ribs as Father Gavriil's voice sounded beside me—strong, confident, divine. Right before his dagger crunched through my chest.

I might have forgiven them—passed on to whatever came next—had I not heard them laugh as my blood pooled to power their workings.

They'd sought to summon a God; my blood paving the way for an immortal to descend to grant them a boon. Youth, longevity, power. But they'd also summoned something darker—and it slipped into my shell like a naiad into a pond and set my heart beating again, slow and steady as a pendulum clock.

I am still Olya, yet I am also not Olya.

The hoot of an owl brings me back to the graveyard, back to my friend reduced to bones. I should have protected her. I thought if I kept my head down, stayed at my mill and carried on, no one needed to know what had happened.

My friend had thought different. When she eventually drew the story from me, she had sought justice. And they had killed her for it. Dumped her in the woods, like me, but without the pomp and ceremony.

I will keep my head down no more. I snap my fingers. The sound ricochets off the graveyard stones. "He'll have priests waiting. We need—" A smile curves my lips. "*Reinforcements.*"

And I have just the souls for the job.

"Lord Voronin, Lady Melina, arise."

Five feet away, the fresh-turned earth shifts, and the scent of copper fills my nose, metallic and bloody. They clamber from their graves. Lady Melina balances her severed head between her nails, features lax, eyes lost. Lord Voronin is expressionless, but that is hardly surprising: my friend has ripped off his face. Their souls push against mine, straining against the power that pulls their strings. I flex my fingers, tightening the hold on my puppets, and bring them to heel.

"A fitting end don't you think?" I say to my friend, eyeing her shattered ribs. I imagine how they would have cracked under Voronin's boot, snapping like twigs under the pressure of his Gods' blessed strength.

The skeleton's hollow eyes move between the marionettes and me. *You're right: you are not Olya.*

I am more than Olya. I am vengeance: the Dark Reaper's right hand. The Twelve may select their chosen, but so has the Reaper. Her boon will balance the scales. At the thought, the scar on my chest twinges: an echo of the woman I once was. I shove the feeling aside, dusting my hands and gathering my skirts. I am not her. The old me was meek and let the world do to her as it pleased. No more.

"We end this tonight."

My friend nods, her ivory skull glinting in the moonlight. Our killers flank us into the night. In life they were beautiful, bastions of wealth and influence, but now they scuttle after us, my power yanking them across the fields like dogs on a chain. Death was my friend's vengeance upon them. Enslavement is mine. Eye for an eye.

The monastery is a grandiose thing. Stone walls hem the opulence in, but beyond them, the arched roof of the dormitory looms, its shingles a deep, starless shadow against the sky. Further away, the steeple of Gavriil's private church rises into the night. *There*, the dark within me whispers. *That is where he will be.*

We follow the wall, ducking away twice as patrols march past, boots crunching on the gravel path. They never see us. Not even Lord Voronin or Lady Melina who drag their feet. Perhaps they choose not to see. We are the picture of death after all.

At the iron side-gate, my friend slides a fingertip into the lock, popping it open with a grinding twist of metal on bone. We steal across the lawn, past the dorm, to Gavriil's personal Godshome, reserved for his most devout.

I wonder if Matev knows. The thought catches me off guard as we climb the low steps to the double oak doors. *What about his Captain and the rest of Lapachka's guard? How many has Gavriil enthralled with the promise of youth and life everlasting?*

With a twitch of my hand, Voronin and Melina push the doors open.

The church is quiet inside. But I feel him in there. His heart races, along with six others, their staccato beats plucking at my senses.

"Gavriil!" I call.

Silence.

We wade into the hall, my friend's feet clacking on the wooden floor, Voronin and Melina shambling after. Images of the Twelve look down on us from stained glass windows. I stride past Uroda of the land and Morskoi the Sea Tsar, through the pews, putting the murals behind me. One God is not present. She never is. She remains undepicted, her name scrubbed from memory. Dark Reaper we call her. The thirteenth God.

I stop before the altar, before Svarog the Supreme, God of the Sun. A candelabra burns there, its twelve arms scattering light across the raised dais. Behind, a templon wall of filigree gold rises from floor to rafter; a locked door in its center bars entry to the sanctuary beyond—the room where my quarry hides.

Movement snaps my gaze to the wings. Hands twist, spellfire roars out: six blinding arcs of green aim straight for my heart. My power flexes, driving Voronin around me. Bolts thud into the chest of my corpse-shield and a sizzling aroma of cooking flesh fills my nose.

My friend reacts, her skeleton hands curling about the priest's podium, knocking the Book of Twelve to the floor as she wrenches it with a strength she'd never had alive. Wood cracks, splinters, and she hurls it into one of the wings. Two priests go down with it, a third skitters away, but she's upon him like a cat. Her charred-bone fingers strike at his skin, gouging welts through his cheeks. He screams, gurgles, and then falls silent.

Three more arcs of green spit from the opposite wing. I twist, dodging one, and pull Voronin-the-meat-shield before the others. Two more thuds, and a fresh waft of burnt skin. Voronin makes not a noise.

I send in Melina. Or rather, Melina's head. The priests scream as a flick of my wrist sends it bowling into them. You'd think they'd be used to seeing death in this corrupt house, but they scatter like crows, cawing for their master: "Father Gavriil, do something. Stop them!"

Still their master does not show. They are alone. Melina collects her head, and my twitching fingers command her and Voronin to advance. They close in, nostrils flaring, scenting the fear that lays thick and heavy in the air.

One priest yells, fires a bolt of spellfire at Melina, then charges between her and Voronin, fleeing down the hall and out into the night. The other two follow, a second strike reeling Voronin back as he reaches for the man. The last priest's spell chokes short as a smoking Melina grabs his arm and tosses him into the pews, as if he were no more than a rag. He slams into chairs with a meaty thud and is still.

A *tap-tap-tap* signals my friend returning to my side, skirmish completed, bones dripping blood. Three crumpled priests lie behind her.

"Can you deal with them?" I motion to the open door and the men fleeing across the grass.

My friend's skull swivels, sightless eyes fixing on the priests' fluttering robes. *Consider it done.*

"Go with her," I instruct Melina. And after the briefest of pauses, in which I tighten my strings, she lopes off, swinging her head by its hair like a cudgel.

I turn to the templon wall and its door. A surge of power crumbles the lock in my fingers, and I push it open. It is dark beyond, a pitch that even my gifted eyes can't penetrate. I gather the candelabra

from the altar and step over the threshold, Voronin poised at my shoulder.

My feet swish over rush matting, the reeds woven into a façade of humility. A musty scent cloys in my nose, reminding me of my farm's old cobwebbed cellar. My chest tightens. I've not ventured into my cellar once since my rebirth. I no longer feel hunger. Or pain. At least, not like I once did.

Thump-thump-thump-thump. His heart is racing. Breathing short and shallow to my ears.

I hold the candelabra high and the shadows pull away as I peer into the gloom. A flash of gold lacing draws my eye. A robe––and it's occupied. My light illuminates Gavriil's face, white and sweaty, his forehead creased with lines of fear.

White light flares, blinding my vision.

"Back, mancer, by the light of Svarog!"

I twist Voronin's strings. He lunges, barrelling straight for the father. The spell takes the corpse in the chest with a heavy *whump,* and I clench my teeth as the Gods' blessing buffets the cords that bind him. Then the light is gone, and my shield slumps to the ground, obliterated beyond recognition.

"Svarog will smite you, foolish woman." Gavriil scrambles to his feet, lips pulling back into a sneer. "The light will prevail."

Not yet. I will not lay down and die, not this time.

I grit my teeth and pull on Voronin's soul, wishing him back up. The corpse rises to one knee. One arm remains, although his head and most of his chest are gone. But my power snags. I draw harder. Voronin's body sways. With a strangled gurgle, my strings break, snapping like spider threads swept up in a broom. Voronin's soul flees. His corpse flops to the floor, still.

Garviil laughs. "Is that it? Is that the best

you have against the true lord's power?"

I stare at Voronin, horror crawling into my chest. I am nothing without my puppets. One single spell, one strike, and he's destroyed my only weapon. The Gods' blessing rises within Gavriil again. A blessing bought with *my* blood.

His fingers weave the spell and fling it towards me. "Die!"

I dive to the floor. My candelabra spills onto the rush matting and fire wicks across it as if it were oil. The spell singes my back and I come to my feet, slapping out a flame caught on my sleeve.

But Gavriil's ready. A second spell rips into my side. Its heat sears my bones and I scream. *So this is the power of the Twelve.*

When I open my eyes again, I'm slumped on the floor. Charred matting burns my skin, smoke clogs my lungs and fire licks the tapestried walls. Garviil's still laughing. He prances about the dais, grinning to the molars, eyes rolling in his head.

"*That* is what I'm talking about!" he cries, throwing his arms wide to the Heavens. "I am blessed; you cannot harm me. Nothing in this world can!"

My fingers curl into the ruins of the matting. The fire's spreading. With every ember that drifts down, flames spring up in its place. I am running out of time. *Damn you, Gavriil.*

As if perceiving my thoughts, he comes, leering through the smoke to wrap a hand around my throat. His touch is a blight on my skin. It sends pain stabbing into my head, behind my eyes. I twist and kick, claw at his fingers. He brushes me off and squeezes, giving himself over to that base desire I'd sensed in that clearing months ago.

Nothing has changed. I bite the inside of my cheek to stop the sobs. My vision narrows to a pinpoint. My heart thuds its slow and steady rhythm.

Thump.

My friend's death will go unavenged. And mine. It leaves a bitter taste in my mouth. I spit a curse, reach up and dig my nails into Gavriil's cheek, sinking them deep. *Something to remember me by, bastard.*

Thump.

I tried. At least I can tell my friend that when we meet on the other side. When I go, the power tethering her to this world will go with me.

Th-thump.

My heart strikes my ribs like an anvil. Something pulls at my limbs, a tightening around my soul. I snap my eyes open. Of course. Why had I not realised?

I reach for the dark, for the other-Olya, within me. She surges, alive, lithe, and hungry at my beckoning.

I am with you, she says.

I'm not a soldier. I'm not one of Lapachka's men of arms. I'm no warrior of legend, or priest of the light. Without my puppets, I have no power to match that of Svarog. I am just a miller's daughter, a widow. One human soul.

But my soul is tethered, too. And my strings call to an unnamed God.

I close my eyes, unfurl my senses, and let not-Olya pull my cords.

We slam our head into Gavriil's. There's a crack of breaking cartilage and he falls away, screaming, blood streaming from his nose.

"Bitch!" he snarls. The light's blessing rises within him again.

We move together, the Reaper and I, weaving around first one bolt then another, the burn of their light dulled through my eyelids. We pirouette and leap, crossing the flames on toe point, alighting at Gavriil's side.

"Stay back!" he screams, scurrying away. "Svarog will burn you to ashes!" A dagger flashes before us. We duck its swing and lean in.

"Svarog cannot help you now." The name stings my tongue and I savor it; savor this moment.

Because I have a dance. *And I also have a name.*

And to know the name is to know death herself.

I whisper it in his ear. The power of it tingles on my lips.

My patron laughs and surges forward, scythe swinging. She severs his soul from his body, and it leaves him in a hush of collapsing lungs. With a brief, muffled scream, her power envelops it and devours it whole, never to see the world again.

Gavriil's body sags, and the dark settles, sated within me. Around us, the Church of the Twelve burns.

* * *

My friend finds me in the graveyard at dawn. Melina skulks behind her, obedient as a hound.

It is done.

"Good," I purr, watching the smoke cloud plume above the monastery.

I help her find her grave. The gaping hole of raw earth is still there, snow stained black from her passage the first time I resurrected her; the first time I heard a soul crying out from beneath the dirt. A soul wronged, like mine.

She clambers in, rests her head on a pillow of soil and crosses her blood-stained bones over her ribs.

May the dead dance for you again, dark one, she says.

I nod.

She goes quietly. Bones slumping, skull lolling, her jaw dropping half askew. The ache in my chest eases a little, like a piece of me has gone with her. I stand there, thinking of the woman she'd been, of the life she could have had. Wronged like me but now silent and peaceful.

I am not silent—or peaceful. But perhaps, as I put more to rest, I will be.

"Come." My power coils about my servant, lurching her up. "This is just the beginning."

Others in Lapachka have sought the Gods' blessing. I know because there were six other sacrifices after mine. Six more souls wronged—maybe more. I know because not-Olya still curls inside my steady heart, sleeping, but not gone. Not yet. We have more work to do.

But how deep will this warren go?

My fists clench. I will hunt them down. And with each of the murdered avenged, perhaps I too may know peace. I turn to the next grave, read the name; listen to the cry of the wronged soul within. I reach out and gather its strings.

"Arise."

COLONY COLLAPSE
BY TOM DULLEMOND

You remember reading about Colony Collapse Syndrome during your studies. There's a whole school of thought among the locals about how the decline of key pollinators spells the end of agriculture. If you extrapolate that to hives in general—worker drones disappearing, leaving only a queen and some nurses and larvae—then the loss of America starts to make sense. You saw the news footage of fires and panic, and you're glad none of that is happening in Australia.

Not that you've ever been to America—you and yours are sixth-generation Sydneysiders, resident since the 2000 Australian millennium celebrations. You've seen pictures of that party, even though it was years ago and before your time. There's a joke doing the rounds that you're basically locals now. You don't think that's very funny.

The road heading into the regional town of Dymballa is unlit, but bright town lights pinprick the horizon against the black night. You're not feeling great. But that's ok: you just have to hold it together until you finish this shift. Everyone always says if you work too hard you fall apart, but you have a whole year left so why not achieve something with your life, right? Family, friends—those things are important, but you don't have to surround yourself with them all the time. Plenty of space to spread out in Australia. Crawling over each other in Sydney for want of living space isn't the life you envisioned.

"You hear that?" you yell inside your rental car, as you ride the speed limit and hurtle closer to the Dymballa shop of Deliciosa Pizza, now cresting the horizon with an orange neon-lit triangle wedge and pox-marked dots that are supposedly slices of salami. It's a logo designed by an infant who understands the concept of pizza but not the essence of it. Pizza as message, not medium. There's a twinge in the stomach and you try not to let out a burp. "JUST HOLD IT TOGETHER!"

You spasm, and it turns into coughing by the time it works its way up and out. A beard with mucus is not a good look, so you carefully wipe it away and check for presentability in the car rearview mirror. Beard smoothed and now mucus-free. Face a bit yellow, but that'll be the stomach problems, and there's nothing more you can do about that.

You pull up outside Deliciosa Pizza. The parlour is surprisingly busy for early evening, with faces visible through the windows, bobbing over meals. The rental car's engine shudders as you turn it off. It's old—older than you, a 2010 model a grandparent recommended—but it came cheap. Good old petrol engine: none of those modern hybrid electronic pieces of crap. 'Built for passenger safety' has never been much of a selling point to you.

You grunt as you shove the door open with a knee and step into the cool night air. Your suit does not fit you well. There's a kink in your spine and it's so tight in there that you can't even twist to relieve the tension without doing more damage to yourself. Biology was never really on the study schedule for you beyond the necessary basics of which holes are for what (*there's a sex joke, you think, and try to laugh but you're just huffing air out and making* yourself more uncomfortable now). Biology is not a terribly useful way to approach your true love: economics. That entire Colony Collapse article was interesting to you as an economics metaphor and vague warning about management hierarchies, more than anything. Real colonies are like well-organised corporations, self-managing teams with a flat hierarchy. Kind of the opposite of a franchise or shitty little wannabe pizza place like Deliciosa.

You slam the car door and walk slowly across the carpark, adjusting your jacket and carrying a briefcase. The briefcase is just for show: an old-school accessory for management types. There's nothing useful in there; no paper because you never bothered learning to handwrite, and no electronic gadgets because they're such a hassle to carry when you're not working and there's never any coverage between towns anyway.

You walk in through the doors. They're immaculately cleaned, with none of the outside world's dust streaking the glass. Some dedicated workers here for sure, which is going to suck for them because they're all going to be let go.

A bunch of locals is sitting around spotless beige tables with brown wooden trim. There's a flatscreen television on one wall, muted, showing CNN and more American news, which you try to ignore. An American local is being interviewed. He's holding up a charred corpse like a trophy. It's small, maybe two years old, and broken in too many places. There's a Trump quote about fire and fury in the report's chyron.

You turn away in disgust.

The entire venue is branded with three colours—orange, beige, and brown. You've never seen these arrangements before, and you're an expert on pizza establishments

so that makes it clear to you that this is an independent organisation. Since your job is to acquire independent organisations, that means the drive out here wasn't entirely pointless. And your family told you there wouldn't be any pickings out this far!

This is why you're a regional manager for a respectable family-owned business, not a corporate drone trying to convince shareholders to vote against their best interests. Shareholders! The notion of public shares is ridiculous short-term thinking, and you would know because you studied the way the planet works. Capitalism. Dog-eat-dog. And so forth.

Pizza-eat-pizza! You try for a friendly smile, think you get it right, and head for the counter.

"Good evening," says the teenage boy, dressed in a Deliciosa uniform with beige cap. "Are you eating in or…?" A nametag with the lop-sided Deliciosa logo on it reads, 'Petr'.

"Not tonight," you reply, looking him over. He has a glazed look in his eyes. "Just interested in management. The name's Karl." You keep your gaze fixed on his and reach out a hand. It trembles only slightly, which means you're getting better at this.

The pizza drone looks at you, then slowly down at the hand and back up.

"You from abroad?" you ask pointedly.

"Uhh, originally, yeah?" he replies.

There's movement from the locals. You spot it out of the corner of your vision and when you turn to look you feel a tightening in the chest, one of those reflexive moments of recognition, at the sight of a young girl.

"Daddy?" The girl approaches a little hesitantly. "You're back! Are you working?"

"Sure," you say, trying to look away.

"Daddy, you were on holidays for ten days!"

"It's very busy work, my darling. But I'll be in town for a while, I think."

She stands there a moment, so you say, "What pizza are you waiting on?"

"Uhm, Mumma likes the seafood one." You look up. A woman is watching the both of you from a booth, so you wave quickly but look down at the girl and say, "Just go back to the table and I'll make sure it's ok."

The Deliciosa employee hasn't moved. He's not doing a great job of fitting in with the clientele, but to be honest you didn't expect a small-town shop like this to really have its shit together.

You've had enough and step around the counter, heading towards the kitchen door.

"Ah sir?" says Petr, trying to grab your sleeve as you move past him. "You can't go back there, that's restricted space for the manager."

You stop, turn, and look him in the eye. Really in the eye. It's a stare that says *look, we both know what's going on here and I'm taking charge.* The type of stare that promises violence. And there are broad shoulders under your jacket. You raise a hand and curl a fist—slowly, but visibly.

There's no negotiating, really. You turn away and push through the kitchen swing doors before he can respond. It's dirty here, the opposite of the clean, inviting entrance. That makes sense from an efficiency perspective, but it's sloppy management. Stainless steel ovens line one wall, tubs of ingredients the other. Fresh out of the ovens, four steaming pizzas are laid out on a bench. The kitchen takes a left corner out of sight at the back, where it's darkest. There's no one else here that you can see.

You lean over the food, and although you feel only revulsion there's a reflexive welling of saliva as flavour and heat surround you. You wipe it off with your sleeve.

That's when you hear movement from the back of the kitchen, just out of sight around the corner, and that's when the worker barges after you into the kitchen.

"Sir, you—"

You straighten up and face him.

He stops nervously at the entrance. You raise a warning finger, and walk slowly backwards to where the kitchen turns, to where the sounds are. Is that where the manager is hiding?

When you reach the corner, you glance quickly to the right, taking in as much information as you can in the dim lighting. Three locals, fully dressed but dishevelled, are chained to the wall, gagged. They're bruised and a little dazed, and by the look of them they must've been here for a few days. Their eyes widen with hope when they see you, and they struggle a little against their chains.

"Sir…" says Petr, plaintively. "You can't be back here. I'll get my manager."

"Oh, yes please. You do that."

His face is still blank, but you feel like he might be trying to narrow his eyes at you and failing. You nod.

While he carefully kneels to rummage through one of the open benches nearby, pulling out a large wicker basket, you return to the pizzas and lean forward, leaning both hands on the bench for stability. It's time.

Still leaning over the pie, you grip the stomach with six of your legs, squeezing and massaging so the suit gags and convulses. The mucosal egg-mass that has been putting so much uncomfortable pressure on the stomach pulses up and out through the oesophagus, slopping in foamy strands from the mouth and onto the pizza base, slipping between ridges of tomato paste and mushrooms and shrimp and slowly settling into the pie's valleys. Sharp tendrils of pain run up and through the entire nervous system, but you pay them no heed. *I can hold it together a little longer.*

You stand again, turning to face the scared worker who's now carrying the manager's basket, and before you can say anything you give him that stare again. There's not much chance that Petr-the-drone is going to argue with someone who just brazenly deposited an entire egg-mass on his pizzas. In the basket, the manager lies coiled, no longer than a two-year-old; flat, millipede-legged, and chitin-slick. She hasn't worn a local in months, probably. Her carapace is the same orange, beige, and brown mottle as the pizza parlour. Your family is black, grey, and crimson, but try fashioning *that* into a local-friendly fast-food brand.

"Consider this a hostile take over," you say. The tongue is swollen from the violent expulsion, but the drone can hear you clearly and will relay it to the manager. She can't understand local language anyway like this, and it's not like you're giving up even this ill-fitting suit while there's work to be done. "I will let you two head into the desert; there are wallabies and all sorts of large mammals out there. Stay away from the locals and don't fuck up. Remember what happened when colonies were exposed in America."

"Uhh, ok," he mumbles.

You think he might try something desperate.

"Don't try anything," you say. "I'm four years old." You let the weight of that sink in. He's what, maybe a six-month broodling? You studied for weeks to get this job. You've been clinging to the inside of this suit for ten whole days, mandibles clenched on the medulla, spine stretched through the torso and ribs, most legs uncomfortably coiled around nerve and muscle, spare legs cradling the stomach and lungs and all the complicated primitive shit that makes up one of the locals. You're in no mood at all for any pushback.

He's old enough to know when he's outclassed, at least. He wobbles slightly under the bulk of the ex-manager's basket—the stress of losing his colony obviously affecting his ability to control the local he's wearing—and staggers out through the exit door.

You brush your jacket off, wipe the face with a rag, and grab a pizza cutter to slice the pies. Simple, honest work. You plate the orders and bring them out to the waiting locals, winking at the daughter, who stares long at the face. You try a smile, but the suit is not happy, not happy at all, so you force a smile.

"Enjoy!" you say, before heading into the kitchen. The chained-up locals are probably incubating workers. They're going to need to be assimilated. It will be messy, but it's not all bad: this ill-fitting suit has a few days left in it, then you'll have the chance to take some days to yourself, slough it off, and really stretch out.

Later, when Dymballa is established, you'll catch a ride with one of the other locals to inspect the next shitty independent pizza parlour down the line.

Fuck indies and franchises. Family-owned is where it's at.

A CHARM TO SICKEN
BY JULEIGH HOWARD-HOBSON

You will need to leave an egg out under
The hot sun for two weeks before you make
This. Carefully, place the egg on yellow
Cloth (cut a square from a sickbed sheet for
More power), add your target's hair, then take
A piece of yellow string and tie it, slow
And steady—don't break the egg. Dig a hole
With your right hand, carefully place the charm
In it. Spit on it three times. Sprinkle this
With water taken from your toilet bowl.
Cover it—gently. Lift your foot. Say: *"Germ*
And dirt, harm and hurt, transmit your foulness!
Infect the body, bring disease! A swamp
Of fever now released!" Drop your foot. Stomp.

HIDEOUS ARMATURE
BY JOANNE ANDERTON

"You want him to look like he's sleeping?"

I push my glasses up my nose. "You realise, if you do that, he'll look dead?"

"She," he client says. "Faust is… Faust was…a she." Young guy, mid-twenties, long hair in a bun, and tattoos down one arm. There's redness in his eyes and on his forehead, and I realise he's been crying. Sweet, I guess.

"Faust was a she." I try to keep a neutral tone. Never judge a man by what he names his cat.

"Sleeping was her favourite thing. In her little bed, in the sun. That's what she'd like to do in the afterlife too, you know. I want her to be happy."

I turn to the laptop. "Sleeping it is."

catch sight of yourself reflected on the screen thin lips colour gone hair falling out sunspots who the fuck did your makeup this morning couldn't contour your fat jowls away could they

Run up a quote and print a waiver for him to sign. There are always extra precautions when it comes to pets. More emotions involved than with trophies or specimens.

"Vet froze her." He talks too much. "Straight when it happened." There's a tremor in his hand as he signs the form and passes me a credit card. "Said it would keep her in the best condition."

Bet they tried to talk him out of it, too. "I'll do my best for her."

Faust is a white domestic long hair with a prodigious fur coat. She's also one of the biggest cats I've ever seen. Not fat big, just large in structure and, I guess, personality. Wouldn't stuff and keep a mediocre cat in her favourite bed in the sun, now would

you?

"You are beautiful," I tell her, as I set her up to defrost. A bed of paper towels on a wire rack with a drip tray underneath, a fan to circulate air, icepacks around her extremities, so they don't thaw too fast and spoil. I keep the studio cold, so the process is gradual, to avoid the slipping of her skin. The chill raises hair on my bare arms, and I lap up the discomfort.

your body reflected in the steel skinning table is bloated and tinged icy blue

I take measurements as she eases into her natural shape, and begin to sketch.

* * *

Hetty's skin is the colour of sugar turning to caramel. I suck her sweetness from my fingers as I stare at her, wrapped in pale blue sheets on the bed beside me. I think I love her the most when she sleeps. Mouth and forehead softened, sweat drying curls into her short hair.

I've learned over the past two weeks that she sleeps soundly after sex. The week before that, I discovered the small cat tattoo on her ribs, just below her left breast. Before that, how wild her hair got if she didn't keep it short. I told her it reminded me of the fur of some beautiful creature, and learned that was not an appropriate comparison. Sitting up, careful not to disturb her, I brush away the dusting of mascara and blush I've left on the pillow, then lean over her face and draw a deep breath. So many more things to learn. I wish I could absorb them like her scent.

Hetty might sleep well, but I'm restless. An electric echo of her skin against mine makes it impossible to lie still. This is something she has learned about me.

I swing my legs off the bed and collect my clothes from the floor. She had wrinkled her nose at them earlier when she opened the door. "Do you have to wear those crusty old jeans?" she'd asked. "What about a skirt once in a while?"

"Do I look like the kind of girl who wears a skirt?" I'd said. Bottle of wine in one hand, boring hair in its usual ponytail, no makeup, scruffy old boots, and rips in my jeans. A bulge in my back pocket where I usually carried my wallet but tonight, I had the camera stuffed in there too. An oversized shirt hid it nicely.

She'd stepped back from the door, letting me in. "Oh, I don't know—"

I'd kissed her cheek and then her lips and leaned my body into hers and hers against the wall.

"—they have their benefits."

"Benefits." I repeat the word as I stand, practise her husky intonation. I could bottle that, get drunk on it. "Benefits." The way her breathing changed as I slipped my free hand beneath her denim skirt and proved her point. "Benefits."

I dig out the camera, then stride naked to my half-empty wine glass balanced on her bookshelf. A cluttered bedroom in a small inner-city apartment block, with wooden floors and cracked stained glass in some of the windows. It suits her. She works for a start-up, writes poetry, drinks coffee at a cafe where they all know her name. As a kid, she took dancing classes and now she's joined a group who do it for fun, once a week in a converted warehouse. She goes to bed early but stays awake late, reading. When she gets her groceries delivered, there's always kale somewhere in the box left at her door.

The more I learn about her the more I want to know. I scan the bookshelf, judge the angle at which it faces the bed. Take a sip of wine. Pick a book, flip through it, put it back. Slip the camera in beside it, lean back, can't decide if it's too visible so take it out. Another drink. Pick up a figurine of a dog, totally fail at hiding the camera behind it. Dismiss the usefulness of a wooden photo frame; pick through a collection of earrings in a porcelain tray and rule that out completely.

"Luci?" Hetty's lifted her head and is peering blearily at me. "What're you doing?"

Shit. Camera hidden behind my back, I kneel beside the bed. "Sorry. Did I wake you?"

"Wanna have a shower? I'll only be a sec."

"No rush," I whisper to her. "Keep snoozing." Cup her head in my hand and kiss her eyes closed.

She turns over and snuggles deeper, holding the sheets to her chin.

I stare at the delicate pattern of vertebrae along the back of her neck. Freckles have snuck in where she can't reach with the sunscreen, her shaved hairline's starting to grow out, the pointed tips at the top of her shoulders slope gently down her arms to her waist.

No more time for indecision. I stand, return to the shelves, and slip the camera in between the two dustiest books I can find, then head to the bathroom. The room is small and needs renovation, with mouldy grout, a cracked basin, and a single mirrored cabinet on the wall.

your skin is not sugar your skin is caked in thick foundation cracking and old and the wrong shade for your complexion

The mirror faces the shower.

the seam down the back of your neck is poorly sewn your arms shoved into your shoulders at the wrong angles

I don't bother with hot water and turn slowly in the shower, shivering until my fingertips go numb.

what's crawling out of your back cats' paws and antlers and tufts of fur slipping over faulty armature can't conceal your sagging face your dead lips the pustules where your eyes should be

Hetty's rolled over to her back, tossed her arms above her head like a halo. Precious little painted toenails peek out from the end of the bed. I stand dripping in the doorway and wonder how someone so perfect can bring themselves to touch someone like me.

* * *

Faust finishes thawing the next day, and I set to work. The temperature in the room will remain cool, fresh air pumped in through vents in the ceiling. My studio started life as a basement, and was the reason I bought this small, 1950s house in the first place. Most people invest in kitchen renovation, or at least rip up the carpet. I did all my remodelling downstairs.

"Already look like you're sleeping," I tell her. Except, of course, she doesn't. Nothing dead actually looks like its sleeping. There's a softening, a lack. Something missing beneath the skin. Something it's my job to adequately replace.

I strip off my clothes—the same jeans, the same shirt, right down to the same undies and bra—and let the cold seep in. The floor is polished metal, like the table, the walls all mirrored and bright in the spotlights.

you see yourself in those mirrors there is no escape

Run fingers through Faust's long, soft fur. The feeling makes me think of Hetty, makes me ache for her touch, her closeness. Biting my lip, I grab my phone and prop it up so I can watch her as I work.

"Weak," I say to myself. I'd planned to wait for longer before I accessed the camera feed.

weak is the least of your worries neck like a pile of bricks something rotting in your left arm green and black and dissolving right to the bone

Blade sharp, fingers practised, I skin the cat. I treat the pelt in a careful chemical mixture of my own devising, to preserve as much of her perfection as possible. All that's left is a fleshy structure, a putrid architecture.

"I'll build you a better one," I promise her. "Equal to your beauty."

tear back your skin go on do it there doesn't it hurt you don't glisten underneath you are just as filthy as on top

Wrap a quick towel around the cut in my arm, tie it down with gauze. Glance at Hetty as I worry it into place. She's just come home, stepping into her bedroom, shedding coat and dropping bag, easing feet out of her shoes. Those polished toes.

I don't need Faust's meat, so I cut her back, all the way to the bone. Her legs and skull will be my foundation stones. Treat them too, clean and polish until they are smooth. Pause to watch as Hetty changes into a short green dress. I know the one. There are little red birds embroidered into the collar. Then I gather the wool and the wire for the armature, my measurements and sketches. While Faust's skin and fur dry, I will build her.

eyeliner trailing down your cheeks cutting you open in its wake seeping over your shoulders pooling fetid on the floor

First, I lay out the bones and mould the wire into a rough draft of a cat. Fill in the gaps with wool. Press and pull, squeeze and cut, build legs beneath my fingertips, haunches, shoulders, little cat knees.

check yourself in the mirror and you like what it's doing to your legs how it redistributes some of the fat to pad out your calves

Most clients ask for lively poses, hunting or sitting or standing tall. Sleeping requires delicacy.

you stop hunching over like a rickety hag and stand tall for once in your life takes some of the focus away from the claws you have instead of hands

The curl of a tail. Fingerprint indents in the plasticine, I build across her skull, defining the classical structures of her face.

jaw reappears and cheekbones form with a nice contouring shade of blush

The room is cold, but I don't feel it. The clock ticks, but there is no sound, no feeling of time passing, nothing but the low creak of wire and wool, the building of a body beneath my hands.

"There we go," I breathe across the mouth I'm modelling. It still needs a plastic tongue, though small and barely visible in sleep I will know it's there. Faust will, too. "Almost done." My breath travels down her woollen throat, right through her armature. "A perfect little body for your perfect fur."

but it doesn't last and your arms curl out of place and fur grows down your shoulders and your feet flatten and spread across the floor

Not perfect enough. Not as perfect as… I straighten, stretch my back and look at the phone.

Hetty's not alone.

* * *

Hetty has the blinds drawn, the light from the bedroom glowing behind the slats. I stare at it through the car windscreen, then back at the phone, then back at the window, then back at the phone. She's sitting on the edge of her bed with a woman I don't know. They're facing each other, knees almost touching. Each holding a glass of white wine.

My legs hurt at the closeness of those knees. Hetty, slender and strong, her dancer's legs. The other woman has messy hair and tattoos, and the knee that is too close to Hetty is pale as the belly of a beached whale.

They drink in sips and they talk. I peer closer to the phone as though that will improve the resolution, but I can't make out the expression on Hetty's face. Are they serious or laughing or flirting, sitting on the edge of the bed, drinking wine?

catch a glimpse in the rear vision mirror you were trying so hard not to look at the sores on your face that you can't hide

I close my eyes. It was only a matter of time before I lost her, but I thought I'd have longer than this. I need her like a hunger, like a thirst. The symmetry of her architecture is air for my lungs.

Open them to see Hetty and the stranger standing. A small step and they are in each other's arms, spilling wine on each other's skin, a deep embrace held so long I'm surprised they don't melt and blend. But then they separate, and Hetty takes both glasses in her strong, steady fingers and the two of them walk out of frame.

I sink down in my seat, watch the window, the front door, the street.

your mouth in the side mirror is a voodoo doll stitching tied into a false smile

It takes far too long, but the strange woman eventually leaves. I watch her walk down the street and clench my hands into fists and breathe through my rage at her swinging hips. Hetty doesn't return to the bedroom. Another long, deep breath. Watch the clock. Give her a minute. Give her two.

Then I'm out of the car and across the road and into the building and up two flights to knock on her door.

Her look of surprise is adorable: large eyes

widen, lips open just a tad. "Luci?" she says my name and I can't help myself, I lean in to kiss those lips. I know I should be angry, but Hetty's smell disarms me. I am willing to forgive.

"Hi," I whisper into her mouth. She tastes like burned sugar.

She returns the kiss, but there's a hesitation, like she's holding a part of herself back. Doesn't she know I need all of her? Without her, I will come apart at my seams.

"Did you forget something?" she asks when she pulls away.

Just what life was like before I met you, I almost say, but her guarded expression, the worry between her eyebrows makes me pause. "Oh, yeah, ah…" I need to ease that look, smooth it down before it leaves a mark. "Realised, my wallet, I think. Must have."

"Really? From yesterday? Did you only just notice?"

I shrug. "Working from home, you know, can be like that. Can go through a whole day and not need anything at all."

She lets me in. "You could have called." Closes the door behind me. "I don't think it's here." Crosses her arms.

"Only be a sec." I head down the corridor, looking over my shoulder, meeting her eyes, trying to draw her with me. Stop at the kitchen. Two glasses on the bench, two different coloured lipsticks on their rims. Stars edge my vision because I can't breathe without her. Doesn't she realise? She's suffocating me.

I pick up the glass that doesn't belong to her. The colour on the rim tells me, the imperfect smeared lips. "Got company?" I ask. I try to sound innocent.

Hetty follows but leaves space between us. "Luci," she says again, "why are you here?"

Try to put the glass down but my fingers are shaking and somehow, I drop it, somehow, I throw it, smashing against the kitchen floor.

"Jesus!" Her arms unfold. "The fuck was that?"

Turn to her. There, that's better. No more reminders of your sneaky bitch-on-the-side.

She swallows so hard I can see her throat move. "I think you should go."

"No," the word escapes me like a dying breath. "Please. I just… I missed you." Lift up my arms to hold her.

"Luci, look, I like you, but you can't just come in here whenever—" She pauses, frowns. "What the fuck?"

The phone's still in my hand. The camera feed still playing. She grabs my wrist, pries it out of my grip and I let her. Don't fight it, don't do anything that could blemish her.

"This is…this is my room." Some of the colour drains from her face. I would prefer it didn't. "Holy shit, have you been watching me?"

"Who was she?" I take a step closer. "Why was she here?" Another, quiet and slow.

"How could you, Luci?" Hetty looks up from the phone. There's terror in those eyes now. "I thought you—?"

you see yourself in her eyes and you know she sees you too the terrible patchwork of your face the seams all split and thread too thick meat bleeds out of the edges nothing you do can to hide what's underneath
your hideous armature

"But I do." The syringe is small enough to fit in my pocket and I pull the cover from it one handed, with practised fingers. "So much." Cup the delicate nub of her shoulder. She lifts her hands and she drops the phone and she's trying to push me away, I think, her touch the batting of butterfly wings, as I slip the needle into her skin. Draw no blood, leave no scar. "You are perfect. How could I not?"

She sinks into me. Sleep softens her face.

I carry her to the bedroom, lay her down on the pale blue sheets. Wrap her carefully, arms against her sides, pad and tuck so she won't bruise. There's makeup on the pillow I slept on last night, a smear that won't rub off no matter what I do. I flip it over, collect Hetty's pillow instead, remember to retrieve the camera and take them both down to the car. Set up a little bed for her in the backseat. Then wait. Wait for the restaurants, the café-turned-bars, and the late-night galleries to shut their doors. Watch the thin mid-week crowd at the pub down the road dissolve, the pokies quieten, and the lights go out. I don't dare risk it, not yet, not until the pawn shops and the sex shops give up, too. Just before dawn, that darkest of moments when the world pauses, only then do I collect her. She's light in my arms and warm against my chest as I carry her to the car.

* * *

They lie beside each other on the silver table, asleep as I fit their skin. I start with the cat. Faust's thick coat makes it easy to hide the seams. There are no such shortcuts with Hetty.

Faust fits her armature perfectly. Her new body is wool, wire, and plasticine, layered around her bones. Her limbs are elegant, paws petite, the mane of her thick, rich neck falls in pale crests across her shoulders.

you sneak glances at the mirrored walls as you work to see your legs solidify your hands turn from claws into fingers

Two tiny fangs escape her mouth, pink tongue just visible if I look closely. I can almost feel breath on my face, almost hear her snore. Her glass eyes the same yellow-green as the fleshy ones long discarded. I set them in the face I've built around her skull,

close her eyelids but leave a tiny slit open, a shining sliver to catch the light and prove to the world that she is, in fact, sleeping. Not dead.

Stand back. Try to see her as a whole, not just the parts I have made or the skin I have placed. She is Faust. And she is perfect.

but your face remains the same rotting cheeks fallen teeth no eyelids nothing but gaping screaming holes

I needed no sketches for Hetty, no measurements. My hands know her every inch. I build an armature over her bones, use silk instead of wool and silver instead of wire. Pieces of jewellery weigh her down: a palm-full of earrings in her hands, the necklace I gave her on our second date around her neck. For her heart, strips of her own blue sheets, tied and tangled, still smelling of sex.

I move Faust to a bench in the corner, spread Hetty out on the table. Her skin is fragile, thin. I hardly dare to breathe as I align her, terrified I'll spoil her with my indelicate touch. Slowly, I ease her onto her armature.

your skin reforms and cheeks ripen wrinkles and creases and strange fatty lumps all sloughing away

Smooth her down with the softness of my lips, from the largest muscles in her lithe thighs to the smallest nooks, the quiet dark places I mapped so carefully. Seal her seams with my tongue.

gone are the creatures growing out of your back the fur and the antlers and the unnameable things

Implant little plastic nails and paint them. Blow them dry.

hair grows back in stop-motion bursts, thick and longer than it's been in years

She never wore makeup, never needed it, and I'm not going to force her now. Just spread clear gloss over her apricot lips. They open beneath my finger to show straight, white teeth. Run the thinnest layer of oil over her cropped hair, to keep those curls the way she liked them, tight and under control.

your breasts perk the way they are supposed to the peaks of your hips protrude just a little your arse tight and strong you don't mind looking anymore do you because now you start to like what you see

The look in Hetty's glass eyes is taken straight from my memory. Softened, peaceful, on the cusp of sleep. I place them and pull her eyelids down but leave a tiny slit. A shining sliver to catch the light because she is, in fact, just sleeping. Here, with me.

"There." I breathe across the flesh of her mouth and into the silk of her lungs. Her fabric heart quivers. "Aren't you beautiful? Aren't you perfect?"

aren't you

I hold her hand and help her stand. I cradle her and carry her and guide her across the room. Don't dirty those feet on the floor, my love. The corners of this world are sharp and your skin is thin, my love, your seams fragile. Don't risk it. Here, let me help you. I will keep you safe.

you are

At the back of the studio there is a small door that looks like a mirror. I press a hidden panel and it swings open. Behind it, a second door, with bolts and locks and combinations that exist only in my head. I hide them from Hetty as I undo each, one by one. Not that I don't trust her. Not that I don't trust any of them.

The second door opens inward. The room behind it is tiny, dark but for a single nightlight, a plastic star with a smiling face plugged into the wall.

"Where would you like to go?" I help Hetty inside. It's getting a little crowded. "I'm sorry, ladies." I hope they hear the sincerity in my voice. "But it's nice to have friends, isn't it?" We find a place for Hetty. And I kiss their lips, all of them, one after the other in a giddy circle until I run out of air and my head spins. "Loveable." They take so much from me. "You all are."

I am.

Countless glass eyes glitter at me, catching the light in their half-awake slivers, and I listen for a moment to the sleepy murmurings, the words of welcome, before I close the door. Turn. Look at all the versions of myself caught in the mirrors that line the walls.

And I smile, run a hand through my hair, fingers across my cheeks. Turn to admire the length of my legs, strong thighs and narrow ankles. Hands on my hips I measure the narrow lightness of my waist. Tanned skin. I open my mouth and I laugh and I pout and I pose in the mirror as I listen to the voices through the wall behind me and know that they are happy.

* * *

"You were right," I say to the client. "She does look happy."

He's crying openly as he strokes the mane of fur around Faust's neck, runs a fingertip down the bridge of her nose, playfully taps the points of her semi-tucked feet.

"She's perfect," he says to me, between gulps of air.

I nod. Loveable.

I catch sight of myself reflected in his phone as he shows me pictures of Faust in her little blue bed, asleep in the sun. And I give him a smile and I coo the right words but it's not really the cat I'm seeing. It's my smooth forehead and neat hair and the way my eyes look larger, browns deeper, than they ever have before. The fullness of my lips. The definition of my cheekbones. I lap it up, drunk on it.

Perfect. Loveable.

We pack Faust up and he carries her out to his car. Cradles the box like a child. "I didn't think," he says, as he secures her on the back seat, "that I would ever love another, you know. Not like her."

I nod again. I do know.

"But then my mate, he has this cat and she's gonna have kittens and I think, maybe, by then, I might be ready." He slides on sunnies, scratches an armpit. "And Faust'll still be there, thanks to you. So I'm not replacing her. Not forgetting her."

His sunglasses are the reflective kind that usually, I hate. But now I stare into them, unflinching, unblinking, and see myself. See what Hetty has made me.

"As it should be," I reply.

He shakes my hand.

and your makeup starts to run

TRACE A CIRCLE
BY J.A. HAIGH

I wiggled my fingers and the rosella hopped awkwardly from one foot to the other.

It was obvious now, that the left wing was loose, the stitching not quite tight enough to hold it firmly in place. *Annoying*. Always had problems with wings. It was hard to find the time to sew properly, and my little hobby wasn't exactly something I wanted to be caught doing.

The rosella had been out near the old Elgas station, slightly flattened, its feathers gritty with road dust. I'd worked hard to plump out the body with cotton wool, tighten up the joints with stiff thread and wax. No matter how good they were when I started, it was impossible to tell if they were right until I animated them.

Rewrapping the red-feathered corpse, I stowed it in my backpack.

The memorial park was my favourite hunting ground. That time of year, the grass was dry and brown, crunching underfoot like frost. The place was deserted.

There was nothing under the powerlines or along the back fence. Next to the toilet block was a single cockroach, belly-up. Rubbing my hands together, I cracked my knuckles, circled the roach with a fingertip, and gestured for it to move. Watched it twirl like a ballerina on one spindly leg, before a piece of it fell away. Apologetically, I let it be, gently laying it back down.

Scouting along the final boundary of conifer hedge, my ears pricked up at the sound of laughter and kids squealing.

Stretching out on the dry grass to peer through the tree trunks, I saw a pair of lilac sneakers. One of them moved, digging a toe in the dirt.

Rocking back onto my knees, I put a hand on the ground to lever myself up.

That's when then I saw the baby bird. Fresh out of the nest, already gone, it lay, unmoving, just under the dense, lower branches. An army of tiny, black ants already starting to explore it. I stared at it. The temptation of those shoes was too much. I had an audience at last, and no one would ever know it was me. I couldn't help myself.

Leaning to one side, I shuffled a little further under the trees, easing my way in. No matter how I tried to be quiet, the pine needles shifted, whispering my intent.

One purple sneaker edged closer to the hedge in front of me, then paused as if someone had stepped in to listen.

Peering through the thick foliage, I made out a tall girl, solid, with shoulder-length, toddler-blonde hair. A paper crown fell over her eyes, blinding her. She pushed it back, annoyed. Her movements clunky, awkward, like a puppy.

Behind her, on a low deck jutting into the yard, a family cheered, glasses tinkling, as they took turns reading out lame jokes from the Christmas crackers. From somewhere inside the house beyond, kids were racing each other up and down a hallway—quick footsteps then a thud, followed by squeals of laughter. The ideal family Christmas.

I lay there, chewing my lip.

Flicking my fingertips at the dead bird, I threw an invisible halo around it, pushed it to move toward the other side of the hedge. There was a soft crackling as the hatchling resurrected, and it scuttled deeper into the shadow under the pine trees.

The blonde girl ducked, shading her eyes, trying to make out what the sound was. The mass of fallen pine needles was thick and fusty. It would be easy enough to dismiss the rustling as just a scrub-hen scratching around for slugs.

I gave my hands another small twitch, and the tiny chick squirmed out of the leaf litter in front of her. Newly hatched, its yellow throat was wide open. Squawking, it stumbled and rolled to one side, claws grasping at the air to regain balance. I saw the moment it caught her eye, the dopey expression of surprise on the girl's face.

I expected a bit of a squeal at least, but she stayed silent. Kneeling, she crawled through the branches to reach out to it but, as she got closer, the ants swarmed over its pin feathers and she stopped.

Its grey skin was teeming with them now. The bird's eyes—black seeds beneath stretched skin—were sunken. It looked dead. It looked like it shouldn't move and yet somehow it was. *Totally creepy.* I smirked, proud, trying to ignore that hot little streak of cruelty inside me.

The blonde edged back, risking a glance over her shoulder at her family still at the table, and I quickly wrung out my hands, releasing my hold over the bird. Turning back to look at my little Frankenstein monster in the pine needles, she found it no longer moving. Lying motionless and quiet. Dead.

Rubbing at her eyes, she tried to refocus, to clarify what she'd seen. There was the spot where it had tunnelled up and a trail of freshly turned mulch from its tumble, hard to deny.

Shimmying my way back out from the trees, I got to my feet, chuckled to myself.

My humour lasted until the bigger girl barrelled through the hedge, knocking me down, the air crushed from my lungs by the weight of her body on my chest.

She forced my arms above my head and pinned them there. "What did you do?" she demanded.

I squirmed, trying to buck her off. She bent my hand back sharply toward the wrist. "Stop, stop, stop!" I babbled.

The pain eased. "How'd you do it?" The girl looked down at me with a red, curdled face.

"What are you talking about?" I tried to weasel away. "I wasn't doing anything. You looked funny, I laughed..." Her expression instantly made me regret my words. It was a wild, gleeful, vicious look.

"Looked funny, hey?" she said. "See how funny you look with a broken arm."

She had a strong grip. Pressure twisted at my elbow, and I screamed.

From the other side of the trees, a woman's voice suddenly called, "Alice? *Alice!*"

The girl whipped around, leapt off. Shoved her way back through the branches. "Lucky for you," she spat as she disappeared.

I bolted.

* * *

When I reached the orchard on the other side of town, I pushed my way through the wire fence, the long grass, slumped under one of the pear trees.

Alice. *What kind of a name was Alice?* People called Alice should wear headbands and be kind to rabbits, not attack people. It was a simple enough rule.

Nursing my sore arm and feeling sorry for myself, I had a good cry before finally pulling it together enough to head home.

All night, I lay there, imagining that girl replaying what she'd seen. She'd known exactly what was going on and she'd known I was controlling it. Her words 'How'd you do it?' churned in my head. I was sick with anxiety.

* * *

A few days later, I was back at the orchard, working on my latest project, when I heard something whisper through the long grass behind me.

I scrambled to shove the sewing under my bag, keeping the trees between us.

She was even bigger than I remembered.

"Martha, right…?" Alice trailed off with a smile. "That's what your dad told me."

I swallowed, lungs constricting. This girl had spoken to my *dad*? She knew where I lived. "What do you want?" I said.

"Your arm okay?"

"What do you *want*?" I repeated.

She pointed at the bag. "How do you do it? That's all I want to know."

It was the admiration that spoke to me— almost a longing sigh.

So, she didn't like people laughing at her, well, I guess we had that in common. Though, at least to date, I'd never tried to break anyone's arm for it. Rubbing my hands together, I cracked my knuckles. Undecided.

"Promise I won't tell, swear to God." She stared at me, eyes dark, waiting.

Hesitantly, I lifted the bag. This one was a magpie, fresh. Almost done. Just needed to finish the stitching at the side of the ribs, where the wool had gone in.

"I recognised you, you know," she said, dreamily. "Think we met once, a long time back. I remember your dark hair and freckles, and you were just the same, all wide-eyed, like you were scared. I kind of wanted to see you again, see if you still looked the way I remembered." She smiled oddly then, pinching softly at her wrist, and pointedly not looking at me while she did it.

I didn't recognise her. I would have remembered. And she didn't know me. I more got the feeling that I reminded her of someone she used to know.

Maybe it wasn't such a risk. Swallowing fear, I lifted my chin. "I have to finish the sewing," I said, watching her.

"Can I hold it?" she asked.

I offered up the dead bird. The wings flopped backwards, showing its chest and throat. Exposing its heart.

"Cool." Alice traced a blunt finger over the needlework.

My lip instinctively curled. Elfin-faced and uneasily pretty within her tall frame, there was something inherently ugly about her touch that twisted my gut a little. Shaking off the thought, I picked up needle and thread, sat down at the foot of the tree.

She settled alongside, leaning a heavy shoulder on mine. Straight away, I felt smaller, more fragile, beside her bulk.

"Can you teach me?" Alice asked.

I frowned.

"Can you?" she prompted.

I reached out, a hand hovering over her blonde head then plucked a stray feather from her hair. Instantly, it felt overly familiar. I expected her to baulk at the gesture, but there was no reaction. Letting go, the feather tumbled away over the scrubby grass-heads.

"Maybe," I mumbled, unconvinced.

* * *

The hot summer days hung around long after Christmas and everyone in town stayed indoors when they could. The whole place seemed like it was in lockdown.

Except for the whirr of insects, the streets were empty and quiet as I walked to the edge of Alice's farm. I'd shown her a thing or two over the last couple of weeks, but she was always keen to learn more.

She leaned against the fencepost, waiting with arms crossed, and greeted me with a sour expression. "I'm sick of sharing a room," she said.

I'd gotten the picture pretty early that she didn't like to share, but she was stuck bunking with the small cousins, Albie and Luca.

"They breathe all snuffly and thick, it's *dis-gust-ing*."

I shrugged. Not much of a one for talking.

"Come on, then." Alice led the way. Down by the creek, a sheep had garrotted itself on the barbed-wire fence and bled out.

We worked at it for about fifteen minutes. Alice was always eager to get her hands dirty, but she lost patience in no time, so we got nowhere fast.

She held the needle out. "I'm no good. You do it."

I looked at what she'd done so far. She was right: it was bad. The stitches were lopsided and uneven, some small, others big and loose. In places the skin was torn through completely from pulling the thread too hard.

Unpicking the work, I started again.

Alice skidded off down the bank to wash her hands.

I'd just finished the line of stitches, cutting the thread, when there was a sharp intake of breath, and I looked up to find a tall, weathered man frowning at me.

He took in the dead sheep, me with bloody hands and all, and gaped. "What in all hell is going on here?" He exhaled.

I half-straightened. Heard Alice halt a step behind me. A cold wash of dread flooded my chest.

"She wanted to practice, Pa," said Alice, quietly.

I stood frozen. *What did she just say*?

"Martha. Remember? I told you about her."

I moved to take a step back. Alice caught my wrist, keeping me close.

"*This* is Martha?" said the old man.

Judging my scruffy hair and freckles.

His granddaughter nodded, wide-eyed, all innocence.

My legs shook. I wasn't dumb. I knew bad things would happen if people found out about my secret. "But…but…you…" I babbled.

"Now," he said to me, holding up a hand. Shaking his head, he indicated the gory scene at his feet. "Alice has a tendency to jump in without thinking. You're better leaving off this kind of thing, wouldn't you say? Gives people quite the wrong impression. Not exactly *ladylike*, now is it? You go wash your hands." He smiled, nodding toward the creek.

Without hesitating, I put the needle down on the carcass and eagerly headed down the bank. Behind me, angry voices sounded. I swear I heard him say, "This isn't *safe* behaviour, Alice."

Beside the creek, staring at the water snickering over the pebbles, I took plenty of time to scrub any traces of blood away with the fine sand. When I came back, they fell silent.

The grandfather stepped forward again. "Alice generally doesn't introduce us to friends," he said. He glanced at the sheep. Smiled grimly. "You hardly need the practice. Let's hope you're not standing over a body the next time we meet." He paused to look at me sternly. "Make sure you don't let others lead you astray."

Dumbly, I nodded and, together, we watched him go.

Turning, Alice rolled her eyes, slipped a clammy hand in mine, pulled. "Come on."

Cold sweat crept over my scalp, but my face was hot. I tugged my hand free.

"What?" Alice grinned. "He didn't care. I told him you want to be a doctor."

Seeing the unexpected flare of my anger,

her eyes lit up. She bit her lip, reached out to touch my cheek as if pleased. "I always wonder just how mad you could get. You're such a dark, little thing, aren't you?"

I didn't say a word. Didn't bother to pick up my things. Just walked.

Behind me, she shouted, "All that effort and we don't even try to move the damn thing? Serious? Jesus, why waste all your time reanimating birds? Yeah, better run on back to the caravan park where you belong!"

* * *

The sun was rising. The park gradually lit up, dark silhouettes resolving into pine trees and slides. At my back, reassuringly solid, was the boundary fence.

The chain of the swing sang as I rocked, waiting for Alice.

The day before, there'd been a note shoved under my door, suggesting I come get my stuff. It had been a while since we'd seen each other. The morning air was heavy with it.

At last, I caught sight of the heavy, blonde figure crossing the field and stood, uneasy.

Alice carried a limp body in her arms. Even at a distance, her face was lit up like a candle.

As she got closer, I saw the damp hair plastered to the boy's forehead, the slack skin around his mouth and eyes. He was wearing pyjama shorts, the fabric thick with water, and runs of it trailed down his skin. He wasn't sleeping. *Jesus.* It was the little cousin. Albie. I gaped with horror at the babyish hands and chubby feet dangling.

"Oh, God." Instinctively, I reached out to touch, to comfort the boy, but he was already gone. He was so little.

Alice didn't react. She was glowing. "This one's all mine," she announced, proudly. "No stitching required."

I shook my head, mute, trying to understand. *What?*

Alice set Albie down, leaning him lopsidedly against a tree, and stood back to stretch her arms. Then she rubbed her palms together. Cracking her knuckles, she traced a circle in the air above the boy's head and tried to move him. She'd been practising. His shoulder twitched, jumping like a rabbit, and I screamed.

A hungry grin flashed across Alice's face.

Another voice called through the dawn, as the pillar of their grandfather rounded the park hedge.

"Albie!" Quickly crossing the distance, he pushed Alice aside, dragging the little one upright. The boy's legs were still pliable enough to sag. "What did you do?" he bellowed, turning on his granddaughter.

Alice's face drained of all its earlier colour and light. Silently, she lifted an arm and swung it round to point at me.

But the old man gripped Alice's head, forcing her to face him. "What. Did. *You.* Do?"

Her dark eyes rolled back like a spooked horse. "Nothing," she whispered, "nothing."

The old man bundled the tiny body to him. Hand lingering on the bare feet, he paused, breathless.

"He wet the bed," offered Alice, stupidly, by way of explanation.

Her grandfather knelt, blinking slowly. I could see his jaw quaking. "What?"

"I put him in the bath."

Silence.

"He must have fallen asleep."

"Liar."

Alice got to her feet wearily, chin weak. "I'm misunderstood."

Taking a step back, I rubbed my palms together, sticky with sweat.

The morning light was a pale grey now, lightening to butter. Against that dawn backdrop, I saw the sharp profile of my sewing scissors, clenched in Alice's hand.

There was the wet thud of metal in meat, as she drove them into her grandfather's back.

The old man jerked forward with the force of the blow, and little Albie tumbled loose to rest in the grass. Sobbing in shock, the old man scrabbled to reach for him. As he tried to turn away, to shelter the body of his grandson, Alice raised the scissors again.

Sickened, I cracked my knuckles and drew a fresh halo in the air over Alice's head. Pulled tight.

There was the squeak of grinding teeth. Alice clenched her jaw, trying to resist. Fighting against her own white knuckles as the point of the scissors turned away from her target, toward her. She twisted to look over her shoulder at me, glaring with suspicion: the sensation must have felt oddly familiar.

There was no question, it was harder with living flesh; one will instinctively fought another. But it worked. After all, I'd been doing it for a while now.

I wanted to vomit, but I made sure to look straight back at Alice, hold her gaze.

Oh, I could teach her something alright.

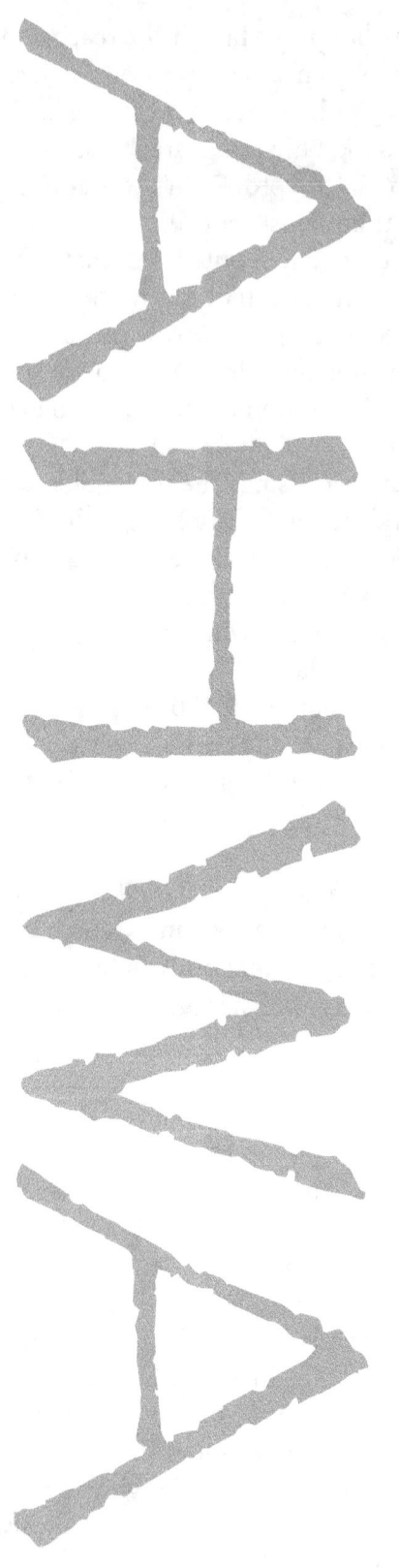

GUEST EDITOR

LEE MURRAY is a multi-award-winning writer and editor of science fiction, fantasy, and horror (Sir Julius Vogel, Australian Shadows) and a three-time Bram Stoker Award® nominee. Her works include the Taine McKenna Adventures, collaborative series the Path of Ra (co-written with Dan Rabarts), debut collection *Grotesque: Monster Stories*, several books for children, as well as stories and poems in notable venues such as Weird Tales and Space&Time. She is proud to have edited fifteen speculative works, including numerous award-winning titles. Co-founder of Young New Zealand Writers and the Wright-Murray Residency for Speculative Fiction Writers, she is HWA Mentor of the Year 2019 and an NZSA Honorary Literary Fellow. Lee lives in Tauranga where she conjures stories from her office overlooking a cow paddock. Read more at https://www.leemurray.info/ She tweets https://twitter.com/leemurraywriter

CONTRIBUTOR BIOGRAPHIES

JOANNE ANDERTON is an Australian author who, until recently, was living and working in Japan. Her spec-fic includes the novels *Debris*, *Suited* and *Guardian*, and the short story collection *The Bone Chime Song and Other Stories*. She has won multiple awards including the Aurealis, Ditmar and Australian Shadows Award. Her children's picture book *The Flying Optometrist* was a CBCA notable book, and her non-fiction has been published in Island Magazine and Meanjin. You can find her online here:http://joanneanderton.com

JAY CASELBERG is an Australian writer based in Germany. His work—poems, short fiction, and novels—has appeared around the world and been translated into several languages. From time to time, he gets shortlisted for awards. More can be found at http://www.caselberg.net

TOM DULLEMOND is a Dutch/Australian author of weird stuff, mostly short fiction. He has sold stories to magazines like Antipodes, Betwixt, Aurealis and SQ Mag, as well as sundry anthologies across the globe. He writes a regular science fiction column for the CSIRO's Double Helix magazine and is co-director of the writing management site www.literarium.net. Chase him down on twitter @cacotopos.

ANTHONY FERGUSON is an author and editor living in Perth, Australia. He has published over forty short stories and non-fiction articles in a range of magazines and anthologies in Australia, Britain and the United States. He wrote the novel *Protégé*, the non-fiction book, *The Sex Doll: A History*, edited the short-story collection *Devil Dolls and Duplicates* in Australian Horror and coedited the award-nominated *Midnight Echo* #12. He is a committee member of the Australasian Horror Writers Association (AHWA), a submissions editor for Andromeda Spaceways Magazine (ASM) and has been a judge for the Australian Shadows Awards. His works have been shortlisted for both the Aurealis and Shadows Awards. His latest book, *Murder Down Under: Australian Serial Killers*, will be published by Exposit Books in 2021.

JASON FRANKS is the author of the novels *Bloody Waters*, *Faerie Apocalypse*, and *Shadowmancy* and the writer of the Sixsmiths graphic novel series. Most of his work, in prose and comics, falls into (or out of) some combination of the horror, fantasy, science fiction and comedy genres. Franks' books have variously been shortlisted for Aurealis, Ledger and Ditmar awards. In the mortal world, he works as a software engineer and data scientist. Find out more at https://jasonfranks.com

REBECCA FRASER is an Australian author of genre-mashing fiction for both children and adults, whose short fiction and poetry has appeared in numerous award-winning anthologies, magazines, and journals. Her first novel, a middle grade fantasy adventure, was released in 2018, and a collection of her dark short fiction is due for release in 2021 (both through IFWG Publishing Australia). To provide her muse with life's essentials, Rebecca copywrites and edits in a freelance capacity, and operates StoryCraft Creative Writing Workshops for aspiring authors of every age and ability…however her true passion is storytelling. Say G'day at writingandmoonlighting.com Facebook @ writingandmoonlighting or Twitter/Insta @becksmuse

J. A. HAIGH was raised in the wilds of Tasmania and her writing is full of magic and myth. Her work has been published in such places as *Kill Your Darlings*, *Aurealis*, *ASIM*, and *Syntax & Salt*. She currently resides in Newcastle, where she scrabbles away at her dark fantasy novel, while juggling two delightful rug-rats and their witty father. You can follow her at https://twitter.com/southern_dark

MELANIE HARDING-SHAW is a speculative fiction writer, policy geek, and mother-of-three from Wellington, New Zealand. Her short fiction has appeared in publications such as newsroom, Daily Science Fiction and *The Best of British Fantasy 2019*. Her Censored City near-future thriller novelette series is available on Amazon and Book Depository. You can find her at www.melaniehardingshaw.com and on Twitter @MelHardingShaw

JULEIGH HOWARD-HOBSON'S poetry won the NSW ANZAC Award and has been nominated for "Best of the Net", The Pushcart, the Elgin and a Rhysling. Her dark works can be found in *Dreams and Nightmares, The Audient Void, Coffin Bell, The Literary Hatchet, The Haunted Dollhouse, Eye to the Telescope, Polu Texni, Abridged Magazine, Illumen, Eternal Haunted Summer, Mandragora* (Scarlett Imprint), *Five Minutes At Hotel StormCove* (Atthis Publishing), and other places. A post-modern ex-pat drop-out, she currently lives beside a dark forest in the USA, with her husband and a dog. The dog may or may not be mortal.

NIKKY LEE grew up as a barefoot 90s child in Perth, Western Australia, before moving to New Zealand in 2016. By day she works as a professional content writer and by night authors speculative fiction, often burning the candle at both ends to explore fantastic worlds, mine asteroids and meet wizards. Her creative work has appeared in magazines, on radio, and in anthologies around the world. Her debut novel, *The Rarkyn's Familiar*—a dark tale of a girl bonded to a monster—is due to be published by Parliament House Press in 2022.

Perth-based author **MARTIN LIVINGS** has been writing short stories since 1990 and has been nominated for Ditmar, Aurealis and Australian Shadows awards. Livings resides in Perth, Western Australia. He has had over ninety short stories published, and his first novel, *Carnies*, was published in 2006, was nominated for an Aurealis Award and won the 2007 Tin Duck Award for Best Novel by a Western Australian. His collection of short stories, *Living With the Dead*, was released in 2012 by Dark Prints Press, and an original story from the collection, "Birthday Suit", won the Australian Shadows award for Best Short Fiction that year. Both *Carnies* and *Living With the Dead* are available now through Amazon, along with his techno-thriller novel *Skinsongs* and the novellas *Rope* and *The Final Twist*. https://martinlivings.wordpress.com/ https://amazon.com/author/martinlivings

STUART OLVER is a medical researcher living in Brisbane. He relishes all things science-related, including a wide range of speculative fiction. His articles and stories have appeared in Aurealis, Midnight Echo and Writing Queensland Online, as well as several anthologies, including *Short and Twisted, Monsters Amongst Us* and *Shelter From The Storm*. His story "What Came Through" won the 2014 Australasian Horror Writers Association Flash Fiction competition.

DAVID SCHEMBRI is an author, artist and genre poet from rural Victoria. He is the author of the horror collections, *Unearthly Fables* (in collaboration with The Writing Show, 2013) and the Australian Shadows Awards-nominated collection, *Beneath The Ferny Tree* (Close-Up Books, 2018). David's short fiction has been published by Chaosium Inc, Horror World Press, Things in the Well and Midnight Echo. His poetry has appeared in several issues of the Hippocampus Press Magazine, *Spectral Realms*, edited by S.T. Joshi. Poetry appearances are also noted within the *Anno KlarkAsh-Ton Anthology* by Rainfall Books, and issue 13 of *Midnight Echo* magazine. Visit his website at: davidschembri.net

DEBORAH SHELDON is an award-winning author of short stories, novellas and novels across the darker spectrum of horror, crime and noir. Recent titles include the novel *Body Farm Z* (Severed Press), novella *The Long Shot* (Twelfth Planet Press), and the collection *Figments and Fragments: Dark Stories* (IFWG Australia). Her short stories have been published in many anthologies and magazines including *Aurealis, Midnight Echo, Andromeda Spaceways,* and *Dimension6*. She won the Australian Shadows 'Best Collected Work' Award for *Perfect Little Stitches and Other Stories*. Her fiction has also been shortlisted for numerous Aurealis and Australian Shadows Awards; long-listed for a Bram Stoker; and included in various 'best of' anthologies such as *Year's Best Hardcore Horror*. As guest editor of *Midnight Echo* 14, she won the Australian Shadows 'Best Edited Work' Award. Her anthology, *Spawn: Weird Horror Tales About Pregnancy, Birth and Babies*, will be published mid-2021. Deb's other credits include TV scripts, feature articles, non-fiction books, and award-winning medical writing. http://deborahsheldon.wordpress.com

ALISSA SMITH has been an enthusiastic reader and passionate writer from a very young age. Throughout her childhood, she was happiest with her nose buried in a book. From Roald Dahl to Stephen King, she is fascinated by the art of imaginative storytelling. Based in Auckland, New Zealand, Alissa is currently editing her first fiction novel and writing twisted tales.

BLACK CRANES
Tales of Unquiet Women

Almond-eyed celestial, the filial daughter, the perfect wife. Quiet, submissive, demure. In *Black Cranes*, Southeast Asian writers of horror both embrace and reject traditional roles in a unique collection of stories which dissect their experiences of 'otherness', be it in the colour of their skin, the angle of their cheekbones, the things they dare to write, or the places they have made for themselves in the world.

Black Cranes is a dark and intimate exploration of what it is to be a perpetual outsider.

With stories by
Nadia Bulkin, Grace Chan, Rin Chupeco, Elaine Cuyegkeng
Geneve Flynn, Gabriela Lee, Rena Mason, Lee Murray
Angela Yuriko Smith, Christina Sng

Praise for *Black Cranes*

"A bloody-toothed smile hidden behind the hand of propriety and social expectation."
— *Pseudopod*

"This anthology has a power to it. An instant classic."
— *Nightmare Feed*

"As haunting and versatile as the Chinese erhu, the stories in *Black Cranes* pluck and bow the strings of the Southeast Asian experience with insightful depth and resonance."
— *Tori Eldridge, author of the acclaimed Lily Wong novels, The Ninja Daughter and The Ninja's Blade.*